THE**MOTOR**NOVELS

Super Stock Rookie
Saturday Night Dirt

SUPER STOCK ROOKIE

WILL WEAVER

Super Stock
Rookie

FARRAR, STRAUS AND GIROUX
New York

Copyright © 2009 by Will Weaver
All rights reserved
Distributed in Canada by Douglas & McIntyre Ltd.
Printed in the United States of America
Designed by Jay Colvin
First edition, 2009
1   3   5   7   9   10   8   6   4   2

www.fsgteen.com

Library of Congress Cataloging-in-Publication Data
Weaver, Will.
    Super stock rookie / Will Weaver.— 1st ed.
        p.   cm.
    Summary: Trace Bonham knows he is fortunate to be offered a chance at
being a paid super stock driver when he is still in high school, but regrets that
he must leave his friends and home track and wonders if the sponsor is
legitimate.
    ISBN-13: 978-0-374-35061-1
    ISBN-10: 0-374-35061-2
    [1. Stock car racing—Fiction.   2. Automobile racing—Fiction.   3. Middle
West—Fiction.]   I. Title.

PZ7.W3623Svm 2009
[Fic]—dc22
                                                                      2008000810

Frontispiece: Photograph © Dennis Peterson

SPECIAL THANKS

Special thanks to my editor, Wesley Adams, and the whole team at FSG in New York; my crew chief, Bill Smith; my driver, Skyler Smith; the Jerry Davis racing family of Bemidji, Minnesota, who run the No. 48 Super Stock; and particularly to Raymond Rehbein, driver of the No. 29r Super Stock and owner of the Speed Shop in Rochester, Minnesota

SUPER STOCK ROOKIE

1

Trace Bonham's phone beeped in his hand. NERVOUS YET?
The text message was from Patrick, who was riding with
Mel in her car.

NOT YET, Trace keyed back.

Trace and his dad, Don Bonham, rolled west on U.S.
Highway 2 at seventy-plus. Right behind were Mel and
friends in her white Toyota. Following Mel was Tyler,
Trace's pit man, alone in his Chevy pickup. Their destina-
tion: Trace's Super Stock tryout at Rivers Speedway in
Grand Forks, North Dakota. On both sides of the highway, flat fields shimmered in the July heat.

His phone beeped again. HOW ABOUT NOW?

"I wish you'd put that damn phone away and get your

mind right for racing!" Trace's dad said sharply. His dark brown eyes threw a glare in his son's direction.

"It's not like you don't get a few calls from Linda," Trace shot back. Linda was his father's girlfriend; Trace's mother lived in Wisconsin.

"True," his dad said. "But I also take care of business. I'm just saying that you don't get a chance like this every day. You have to be ready."

"Like I don't know that?" Trace answered. This Super Stock tryout was a huge deal to his dad. He had been obsessing on it ever since Cal Hopkins, the Late Model points leader and former sprint car driver, had seen Trace win at Headwaters Speedway earlier in the month and invited him to the tryout. Obsessing on that and Linda, a nurse in Detroit Lakes whom Trace had never met.

"For a young driver like you, this is a potentially career-making opportunity—but you have to *want* it," his dad said.

"I want it, all right?" Trace said, sudden anger in his voice.

His father fell silent.

HOW ABOUT NOW? read the text message, this time from Mel's phone.

Trace glanced over his shoulder. Mel—Melody Walters —seventeen, who managed Headwaters Speedway for her dad, was behind the wheel; she smiled and waved with both hands. She wore sunglasses and her usual World of Outlaws cap. Her car appeared to be empty. Mel put her hands behind her head like she was bored with driving, and looked off across the fields. As if on automatic pilot, her Toyota continued straight down the highway.

CUTE, Trace keyed.

A few seconds later, Patrick Fletcher and the other kids in Mel's car popped up and Mel grabbed back the steering wheel. They all laughed like fools, waving and making faces and obscene gestures at Trace like a car-load of patients escaped from the nuthouse. Cute, but annoying. Patrick—whose "gofer" duties at Headwaters included singing the national anthem—got to ride with Mel, while Trace was stuck for two hours with his dad in their big Chevy Tahoe.

"I wish we could have kept this whole thing more under wraps," his father said, glancing into the rearview mirror.

Trace faked a yawn, certain to annoy his dad, and tipped back his seat. Pulling his cap brim down over his face, Trace closed his eyes. Instead of sleeping, he concentrated on the Super Stock practice laps he had done at Headwaters Speedway . . .

"Start out slow. No rush. First you need to get the feel of the car," John Sitz shouted above the engine noise of his own yellow No. 29 Super Stock. From the cockpit, Trace nodded. He was strapped in, buckled down, ready to roll. Johnny Walters had opened the Headwaters Speedway track on a Monday morning just for Trace—so he could get ready for his Wednesday tryout in Grand Forks. Local racing people were like that, like family. If you needed something at the track—a tire, an air compressor, a socket wrench, a coil spring—or if you needed help off the track in order to be ready for race night, all you had to do was ask. Or not. As with a family, everybody who raced at Headwaters knew everything about everyone, and when word got around about Trace's tryout, John Sitz had stepped up to volunteer his Super Stock (he also raced Late Models) without being asked.

Trace feathered the accelerator and checked the gauges: red, blue, and green for oil pressure, water temperature, and fuel pressure.

"All good?" John called, leaning into the cockpit to look at the flat dashboard.

Trace nodded again, impatient to get going.

"Remember, you've got a lot more horsepower than that Street Stock of yours," Sitz shouted, "but don't be afraid of it. Make it work for you. Trust the car."

Trace nodded, half listening. He wondered at what rpm his heart was beating.

"Take a few slow laps to get the feel of the steering and the setup, all right?"

Trace looked down pit row. He flexed his left leg. Sitz's clutch was strung way softer than he was used to. He brought up the rpm for a smooth start—then lurched forward and killed the engine.

John's laughter filled the suddenly quiet cockpit. "Don't worry about it. This beast has a hair trigger for a clutch."

Trace quickly restarted the engine and, with more rpm and a slower pedal release, eased forward down pit row. Idling along at a throaty rumble, Trace felt strange being the only driver, the only car in the pits; everything seemed larger, and farther away. Then again, Trace was glad there weren't any other spectators. He blipped the throttle—and the Chevy V-8 engine barked like a big dog on a short chain. Steering No. 29 to the entrance at turn 4, he rolled up over the embankment and down onto the track. In this car the dirt was way closer—as if he could reach down and touch it.

Crawling around the track at yellow-flag speed, No. 29 was a Thoroughbred racehorse itching to run. By contrast, Trace's Street Stock was an old workhorse. He damn well better make the new Super Stock team; it would be tough going back to his old car.

Johnny Walters, Mel's father and the track owner, sat on his ATV by the exit at turn 3. Trace's father and John Sitz stood next to him, leaning against the big bumper tires, with their arms crossed. As Trace came by on his first lap, his father did not, he was glad to see, give a thumbs-up or wave.

On the straightaway and then on the banked turn, Trace swerved the car left, right, left, as he tried to get a feel for the steering quickener, for the shock absorbers, for the tires. After Trace's fifth slow lap, John stepped forward and waggled his right pointer finger: a little faster.

Trace brought the speed up slightly, intermittently punching the accelerator, breaking loose the rear tires.

The engine's throaty grunts echoed in the empty grandstand. The Super Stock wanted to run; it hated being held down. After a couple of laps at this pace, Trace's back muscles relaxed; his spine began to conform to the seat. He loosened his ten o'clock–two o'clock death grip on the steering wheel.

As Trace approached turn 3, John stepped forward and spun his pointer finger in a quick, tight circle: hot laps!

Trace cranked up the thunder. He took the car into the turn at what he guessed was three-quarters speed. No. 29 hugged the inside bank, then pitched itself out of the apex like a baseball curling out of a pitcher's hand. His old Street Stock leaned, tipped, and tilted through the turns. Most full-framed race cars were happy to be done with a turn and headed down the straightaway; this Super Stock loved the turns—couldn't get to them quick enough.

Trace pressed faster around the track. The more he trusted the car and the setup, the smoother—and faster—he felt. After several hot laps, John abruptly waved him into the pits. Trace turned off the track and killed the rumbling engine. He coasted to a stop.

"Okay," John said. "Looks like you're getting a feel for the car."

"Yeah. I love it," Trace said with a grin.

"Good," John said. "Ready to do some hot laps?"

Trace stared.

"What?" John asked.

"I thought those *were* hot laps."

"You were getting up to speed, kid," John said with a

smile. "But you're gonna have to be a little quicker to be competitive. The important thing is to find a line that works for you. High, low, medium—you be the judge. Take only what the track conditions give you. One night a track will be a dry slick, and the next night it will be rubbered up from lots of water. You've got to *feel* what's underneath your tires, *feel* where the best bite is."

"Got it," Trace said.

"But the key thing to driving a Super Stock or a Late Model is this: Never drive too deep into a turn. Then you'll have to use the brakes, because that's how we all drive normally off the track. On the track, in each corner you've got to find your lift point—when you lift off the gas. Then your goal is to accelerate *through* the turn. You'll have way more control that way."

Trace nodded.

"Now get back out there," John said, slapping Trace upside the helmet, "and drive this sucker like it was stolen."

Trace fired the engine, spun the tires, and surged back onto the track.

Coming out of turn 4, he threw the hammer down. The empty grandstand flashed by on his right—and turn 1 came up fast. Trace resisted the instinct to tap the brake. Rather, he let off the gas sooner than with his Street Stock—then pitched hard into the turn and cranked the steering wheel to the left. The Super Stock swung its rear end wide right. Trace got back on the throttle in a thundering, tire-spinning drift. G-forces pinned him to the

right side of his shoulder harness as the car surged left—
and out through the turn into the straightaway. "Sweet!"
he shouted. But there was no time to celebrate; turn 2
loomed in his visor. Again he threw the car sideways into
the high bank, and again No. 29 slung itself through the
corner. It was like the tires had claws, and the car had
wings . . .

"Trace. Trace—wake up! We're almost there."

Trace lurched upright in his seat. He couldn't believe
it: he had actually fallen asleep for a few minutes. His
heartbeat punched up a new rhythm. A bunch of tall grain
elevators marked the east side of the city—that and the
sudden, rank smell of a sugar beet plant.

"Gross," Trace said, wrinkling his nose.

"That's the smell of money," replied Trace's dad, a busi-
nessman farmer who knew about such things.

As they crossed the Red River bridge and entered
North Dakota, Trace glanced behind. Their little Headwaters Speedway convoy was intact. They passed a few stoplights, crossed the railroad tracks, then made a right turn
toward Rivers Speedway. When he wasn't racing, Trace
came here once or twice each summer to watch sprint car
races. On those occasions he passed through the old stone
archway with the other race fans. Today his father headed
around the back side, to the pit area. Grasshoppers began
to hop and flutter inside Trace's stomach. The empty parking lot, the silent grandstand—it was like nobody was

here. Even the trailer park just across the fence was quiet.

"It was Wednesday, right?" his father asked.

"Yes. The last day of July," Trace said immediately. Then he pointed. Ahead near the pit gate was a youngish black woman talking on a cell phone; she held a clipboard. They drove forward. TEAM BLU SUPER STOCK TRYOUTS read a small sign taped to the chain-link gate behind her. In the background, at slow speed, a Super Stock crawled around the track.

Trace's father stopped at the pit gate and powered down the window.

"Hold on," the woman said into her phone. She looked at Trace's father, then at Trace. "Name?"

"Trace Bonham," Don said.

She glanced at her list, then checked off Trace's name. "Gotcha. Straight on through to the pit," she said with a nice smile. Then she looked at the other cars close behind. "This your entourage?"

"I'm afraid so," Don said.

"Okay, but they can't be in the tryout area. They'll have to sit in the stands," she said, "and no photos of any kind."

"No problem," Don said. Trace was already texting Mel.

"Go on in, then," the girl said, waving them forward. "And good luck."

If little old Headwaters Speedway felt empty during Trace's practice laps, the big Rivers Speedway pit area was a ghost town. No large car haulers. No motor coaches. No long, parallel rows of tractor-trailer rigs squeezed in an arm's length apart. No humming choir of generators. No smells of freshly ground tire rubber, racing fuel, popcorn, and barbecued ribs. No speeding ATVs with stressed-out track officials talking into headsets.

"Up there," Trace said, and pointed. A small cluster of vehicles and people had gathered at the far end, near turn 3. A big motor home with darkly tinted windows sat nearby, along with Cal Hopkins's long No. 42 trailer.

As they approached, faces turned to look. Several sets of fathers and sons, and at least one teenage girl and her dad, stared at the shiny Bonham Chevy. The kids all wore racing suits, tops down and sleeves tied at waist in hot weather, pre-race style.

"I told you, you should have worn your suit," his dad said.

"Don't worry, I'll put it on!" Trace replied.

His dad parked. They got out and walked forward, Trace leading the way. Walk too slow and he'd look timid. Walk too fast and he'd look anxious. Above all, don't look at the competition. But in the end, tryouts were the same everywhere: a bunch of kids standing around, sizing one another up while trying not to be obvious. Here, some yawned and pretended to be bored. Others talked and laughed too loudly. A couple of fathers murmured instructions into their kids' ears, a useless task because each kid was thinking the same thing: *Who looks quickest? Oldest? Strongest? Who has just the right gear?*

This group of teenagers all wore multilayer fire-retardant racing suits. Simpson. ProTech. The suits were well-worn, their colors faded and oil-spotted—which didn't necessarily mean that the kids had been racing for years. Young drivers often wore their dads' old racing suits, altered to fit. The used suits made them look fast just standing still. Nobody would be caught dead wearing brand-new gear.

"Name?" a woman in sunglasses said to Trace.

Trace opened his mouth. His voice croaked and cracked. Quickly he cleared his throat. "Trace Bonham." No one laughed, though from the side he saw a couple of kids look at their shoes.

"You race at Headwaters Speedway over in Minnesota, right?" the woman asked, looking at her clipboard. She wore red lipstick and had zero tan.

"That's right."

One of the loud-talking kids whispered something to another driver.

"Do they wear racing suits over there?" the woman asked.

"Yes, ma'am." There were a couple of chuckles this time, including a smile from the lone girl driver.

"Well, get yours on," the woman said. "We're almost ready to start."

Trace went back to the Tahoe and quickly changed. His father stayed with the group, where the pale-faced woman with the clipboard flipped open her phone. Her lips moved really fast. Trace zipped his suit and grabbed his helmet. As he exited the Tahoe, three more black-dressed people came out of the big motor home. They all carried cameras.

"All right," the lead woman said, "we're pretty much ready. My name is Laura Williams. I represent Team Blu, and I'm in charge here." Her voice, her accent, was not Minnesota or even midwestern—more like East Coast.

"Let's be totally clear on what we're doing today," she continued. "Because of your racing success and your age, you have been invited to try out for Team Blu, which is looking for a young driver—the right young driver."

Her camera-carrying assistants did not look from the Midwest, either. Who wore dark clothes in the middle of the day in July in North Dakota? Plus, they had odd haircuts—the style chopped or else spiky—and their sunglasses had frames unlike anything Trace had ever seen. The girl at the pit gate seemed like the most normal one on the team.

"My goal today is to get a good idea of who in this group is competitive in our driver search," Laura said. "But nothing will be decided today. The first order of business is to see you drive." She turned to the track, where an unmarked Super Stock powered up for a thundering hot lap. As the car surged close past the fence, the woman and her assistants flinched and covered their ears. Trace and the other young drivers watched without moving or changing expressions.

As the Super Stock slowed toward the pits, Laura looked back to her notes. "Each of you will get four warm-up laps, then two hot laps. And while your lap times are important, they are not necessarily the determining factor in who wins this 'ride,' as you call it."

Several of the young drivers glanced sideways at one another.

"Questions?" Laura asked sharply.

There was silence. Then a short, stocky kid with big arms raised a hand. "You mean, the fastest lap times ain't the most important thing?" The kid had a faint drawl, possibly southern Iowa, in his voice.

"Aren't," Laura said impatiently. "And that's not what I said. Lap times are important for everybody, but there are other factors in today's screening process—like good grammar."

The Iowa kid's face reddened. His head pulled down onto his shoulders like a turtle's drawing back into its shell. The rest of the teenage drivers remained expressionless.

"In addition to time trials, each of you will do an interview as well as a photo shoot," Laura continued.

There was silence among the group of drivers; their eyes went to the assistants and their cameras, then to the motor home.

"Any more questions?" the woman asked.

The silence continued. Then the girl driver spoke up. "Who is Team Blu, anyway?" she asked. "I mean, it's the sponsor, right?"

"That's right," Laura said.

"Sponsors have products, like gas or oil or pizzas or whatever. What does Team Blu sell?" The girl had short brown hair, and brown eyes to match.

"Our product is not important at the moment," the woman said. "What's important is that we stay on schedule. We'll draw for the driving order."

There was nothing like a placement drawing to get drivers in motion, and Trace jostled his way into line. As he waited to draw, he found himself behind the Iowa kid, whose suit smelled like an open jar of pickles. Too many hot race nights in corn and hog country, not enough soap and water.

"There's something strange about this whole Team Blu thing," Trace murmured.

The kid shrugged, his small blue eyes focused on the drivers ahead. "Who cares? A ride's a ride."

2

Trace was used to the old-fashioned way of drawing: reach into a pouch, run his fingers through the chips, pinch one—then bring it out into daylight to read the number. Here at the pit shack at Rivers Speedway, he stepped up to a laptop computer on the counter.

"Just click the mouse," the woman said. She was dressed in a faded Donny Schatz No. 15 sprint car T-shirt and was not wearing strange sunglasses; Trace guessed that this was her regular job on race nights.

Trace clicked—number 47—which meant nothing until all the drivers had drawn. This was standard procedure for determining car order in time trials and heat races. Draw a number, then wait to see where it fell. Number 47, drawn from a larger sequence, could be first or it could be last.

When everyone had drawn, Team Blu's Laura conferred with the pit shack woman, who then came out and wrote the draws on the big marker board: 3, 18, 39, 42, 47, 65, 71, 78, 84, 85, 93, 98.

"Fifth—perfect!" Trace's father said. A couple of other fathers turned and looked. They were not happy. He lowered his voice. "The tires will be nice and warm, the engine loose but not too hot, the—"

"Okay, okay," Trace muttered.

His father zipped his lips. Behind them, the Super Stock rumbled off the track and coasted to a stop by the trailer. None other than Cal Hopkins swung himself out through the window.

Trace glanced at his father.

"Team Blu's racing consultant for this tryout is Cal Hopkins," Laura said. "He knows this car. He has tested the car. He and his crew are responsible for making sure it runs right and consistently for each of you drivers."

"Hey, all," Cal said easily as he walked up to the young drivers. In his silver suit, he was much shorter—probably no more than five feet six inches—than he had seemed when Trace had met him a few weeks ago at Headwaters Speedway. Race drivers as a group were smaller-than-average men. However, with square shoulders on a lean frame and a big, genuine smile, Cal had a large presence.

Trace smiled in return and threw a short wave to Cal. Cal's gray-blue eyes glanced at Trace, but he did not wave back or change expression. Trace slowly tucked his waving hand under his left armpit. A couple of the other drivers glanced his way with smirks.

"I want to welcome all of you young drivers to the Team Blu tryouts," Cal said. "I rustled up a Super Stock of my own for today's time trials. The actual Team Blu car is being built as we speak. But trust me, we've got a good ride for you today. I know—I've won a few races in this car myself."

The drivers and their dads glanced at the car, then back to Cal.

"Let's try to make this fun," Cal said. "Be yourselves, drive fast, but stay under control. We need the car in one piece for the next driver, all right?"

The young drivers glanced sideways at one another.

"Each of you will get your warm-up laps, then two hot laps—just like a real qualifying event. The car carries a transponder. Your time will be posted on the main scoreboard—just like in a real time trial. Any questions?"

No one moved.

"All right then, who's first?"

"Me." The kid from Iowa stepped forward, holding his helmet.

"Name?" Laura said, looking at her clipboard.

"Butch. Butch Hawkins."

"All right, Butch, let's do it," Cal said.

There was something weighty about Butch—his burliness, his thick neck, his square chin. Gravity hung heavier on him than on most people. He was the type of kid who'd probably shaved at age eleven, drank beer and worked on combines at thirteen, and moved into his own trailer house on his father's farm at fifteen—the type of kid who was born old.

Butch's dad, likewise squat and square-faced, made sure that his son was strapped in properly: shoulder harness locked, neck collar cinched in place. The dad had thick, beefy arms that looked as strong as hydraulic rams. Cal did the final safety check. As Butch fired the engine, then accelerated confidently onto the track, the father walked away without looking over his shoulder.

The young drivers lined the fence, fingers hooked in its chain links, as Butch took his warm-up laps. When Cal stepped to the edge of the track and flashed the green flag, Butch hammered forward in turn 3 like he had been doing this all his life. As Butch thundered past the grandstand and pitched the car into turn 1, Trace had a sinking feeling—no, more like a dropping feeling, like being on a roller coaster when the car falls forward, leaving his stomach behind on the rails. These kids were all from serious racing families; most of them were already experienced Super Stock drivers.

The scoreboard flashed 17.86 for Butch's first hot lap, then 17.22 for his second. Transponder or not, most of the other fathers held stopwatches.

"Very good, very consistent," Cal remarked, as Butch coasted toward the pit. "Who's number two?"

A tanned kid, small and wiry, with a summer buzz cut, stepped forward. He looked fourteen at most; his cheeks were smoother than a baby's butt. Brown eyes—"cute," the girls would describe him—except for his ears, which were rolled and cauliflowered. He was a wrestler. Probably somewhere around the 117-pound class. The type of kid who won a state championship every year starting in eighth grade.

"Name?" asked Laura.

"Jason. Jason Nelson. From Nebraska."

His voice was surprisingly deep.

"I brought mah own seat liner, if that's owl right," he said with an accent more Texan than Nebraskan. "Helps mah feet reach the pedals." He grinned. A couple of cameras clicked.

"Sure, no problem," Cal said, taking the liner from Jason's father. "Reaching the pedals is a good thing."

When the liner was strapped tightly over the bare aluminum seat, Jason set his helmet on the roof, slipped feet-first through the window, then reached out and pulled his helmet in after him. He did it in one smooth, quick motion—like a chipmunk disappearing into a hole. Trace's grasshoppers skittered all over again.

When Jason finished his first, corner-slamming, hard-charging hot lap in 17.42 seconds, Trace looked at his father—who looked back with a wide-eyed, slightly frozen expression. Trace shrugged a what-can-you-do? jerk of his shoulders, then stepped close to his dad. "Where'd they *find* these kids?" he whispered.

"I was thinking the same thing," his dad murmured. He draped a hand on Trace's left shoulder as they watched the second lap. This time Jason was faster still but got loose in turn 3, and finished at 18.27.

The tryouts continued, with the girl driver, Sara Bishop from Fargo, running a respectable lap at 18.22 followed by a nice 17.84. The first driver, Butch, had gone inside the motor home for his interview; Jason waited with the pit gate assistant just outside. He was chatting and smiling at her; he was the kind of kid who didn't worry about anything. Trace envied him as much for his personality as for his cornering skills.

The next driver, Ben from Wisconsin, was overly aggressive and got high and onto the marbles—the loose dirt—both times in turn 3. He finished well off the pace in the eighteen-second range.

And suddenly, Trace was next. Sara from Fargo had taken off her racing suit and was stashing it away. Slinging her gear bag over her shoulder, she paused close by Trace to watch the Super Stock roll to a stop.

"Turn 3 here gets drier faster when the sun shines," she said softly. "Stay low, in the shadows. That's where the bite is."

Trace turned toward her. She didn't look at him. She had a pug nose, freckles, and a trickle of sweat inching down her temple. She was not half as pretty as Mel, but the older he got, the less he cared about pretty—up to a point, of course.

"Next," Laura called.

Trace headed to the car, his stomach high up in his throat.

"How ya' doin', Trace?" Cal said.

"Good," Trace lied. His voice was about an octave higher than normal. He set his helmet on the roof, then swung his feet through the window. He focused on getting settled in the seat without making a fool of himself. This Super Stock had the same three cockpit gauges as John Sitz's, and a digital tach on the far side. On the right, for quick access by emergency personnel, was the complete power-cutoff switch—the "kill switch"—for use in case of a crash and an incapacitated driver. The worry, always, was high-octane fuel and fire. Next to that was the starter button.

Cal made sure Trace's belts were not twisted and his sternum protector was snapped into place. Hopkins was clean-shaven and smelled of some old-fashioned kind of aftershave. Trace took the steering wheel from him and locked it in place—giving it a good yank to be sure. A driver had only himself to blame if the steering wheel came off during racing action.

Trace's dad handed him his helmet.

"Okay?" his father asked.

Trace nodded again. He couldn't think of any words.

"Hold it loose and throw it hard," his dad said.

Trace managed a grin. It was their old line from little league days at the baseball field, back when he and his father were tight. He hadn't heard that saying for years.

And it wasn't the worst cliché in the world. On his warm-up laps, Trace waggled his gloved fingers on the steering wheel to keep his hands from a death grip. Clench the wheel too hard, and he squeezed away any feel for the track, for the wide, soft Hoosier tires on hard brown clay. Hold it too loose (little worry about that!), and he lost feeling for the turns.

This Super Stock had sharper steering than John Sitz's No. 29, plus it had a lower center of gravity. The engine felt quicker, too. When he flicked the accelerator, the rear tires broke loose like an A note zinging off a guitar string. No way he was ready to run flat-out in this car. If he could keep from spinning out, he'd be happy.

Ahead, Cal waved a closed green flag: one more lap.

"Okay, baby," Trace breathed, and brought his speed.

Not hammer down on the spot. Not 7500 rpm in one surge. Rather, he concentrated on a strong, smooth pull forward, faster and faster, through turns 3 and 4, and around to the swirling green flag.

He pitched well through the first turn, missed his lift spot ever so slightly in turn 3, but recovered nicely and had good speed down the straightaway. His next lap felt better yet, though he got a quarter second squirrelly in turn 4. Still, he felt fast, and his fans from home stood to clap as he flashed by the bleachers. They stood, but didn't jump up and down wildly.

Flipping up his visor to check the leaderboard, Trace saw why: his first lap was an 18.04, and his second, 17.86. This put him just barely ahead of Sara, and nearly a half second slower than the little wrestler kid, Jason. He would be lucky to finish in the middle of the pack.

Braking in the pits, he tossed his helmet to his father.

"Oh well," he muttered as he swung himself out of the car.

"Hey, you looked good out there," his dad said in the same overly cheerful voice that Trace remembered from little league days—the voice his father used when Trace had a bad day at the plate.

"Not good enough," Trace said as they walked away.

His father was silent a moment. "Nice car, though?"

"And then some," Trace replied.

"Well, all seat time is good time," his father said.

"Good while it lasted," Trace said, looking over his shoulder at the next driver getting into the Super Stock.

"We don't know that," Trace's father said. "Remember—there are other parts to the tryout."

Trace looked around for Sara. She stood off to the side with her dad. He was giving her a one-armed hug, and they were laughing about something. She was trim and athletic, one of those girls who had way more going for her than most boys realized. Trace imagined her in some lame after-school job, like working at the Dairy Queen, then saw her in high school, walking down the hallway past the "cool" girls, the beauty queens, who didn't give her a second look. Not that she cared, which probably irritated them no end.

The tryouts only got worse for Trace. Lance from South Dakota turned a 17.11 and a 16.93. Two more drivers also broke the seventeen-second barrier.

"We had a bad draw," Jason's father muttered. "That engine's just startin' to loosen up."

"Track's faster now, too," Butch Hawkins's dad replied without expression.

Both Jason and Butch, done for the day, were over by the trailer in the shade, where there was free food and soda pop. Trace was next.

"So how you doin', Trace?" said the Team Blu girl by the motor home door.

"Good. I guess."

"Glad to hear. I'm Tasha. I'm the coordinator for this Team Blu thing—*coordinator* meaning 'least important person here.' "

"Hey," Trace said (the lamest of all replies, but at least something came from his mouth). They shook hands. Weirdly, his hands were sweatier for this part than they had been for the time trials. It didn't have anything to do with the fact that Tasha was a really pretty black woman— in her early twenties, he guessed. Rather, it was the way the young drivers exited the motor home. Or better, bailed out of it—like school, or detention, or some kind of test was done for the day.

"We're getting there," Tasha said pleasantly, and glanced over Trace's shoulder.

The next-to-last driver was a round-shouldered, red-haired kid with major acne named Lawrence Wilkins. He seemed embarrassed to be here, and embarrassed at turning a pedal-to-the-metal 16.84 and a 16.68. Afterward, he stood over close to his dad, and chewed his right thumbnail.

"What grade you in?" Tasha asked easily.

"I'll be a junior."

"What do you like most about school?"

"Shop class and lunch," Trace said. It was a standard guy joke.

"But you do well in history and English," she said.

Trace forgot the car noise behind. He looked at her. "How'd you know that?"

"There ain't no flies on Team Blu," she said, throwing down a soft, exaggerated drawl, plus a wink. "While we wait, I need to get some stats from you. Let's start with your height."

"Five seven."

"Weight?"

"About 175."

"Shirt size?"

"Large."

Just then the kid from Wisconsin, Ben, exited the trailer in a rush. His face was flushed, and he blew out a long breath that rattled his cheeks. "Watch out! They make you write a paragraph in there!" he said to Trace.

Trace glanced at Tasha, who smiled.

The male assistant to Laura, the guy with spiky hair, poked his head through the doorway. "Next!"

Inside, Trace blinked to adjust to the dimmer light. In the dining area, the table was covered with computers and camera equipment and file folders. Twelve folders, including one with Trace's name on the front.

Trace swallowed and felt his hands go even more

sweaty. Give him 7500 rpm and a quick-lock steering wheel any day.

"Sit," Laura said without looking up; she scribbled notes on a yellow legal pad.

Trace obeyed.

When she finished, Laura tore off the page and inserted it into a folder (Ben's).

"Okay!" she said brightly, and turned to Trace. She looked him up and down for a long moment. Then she handed him a page from a magazine, the kind with no pictures. "Read this to me, please."

The title was about global warming. "Aloud?" Trace asked.

She waited. Trace put the page on the table so it wouldn't shake in his hands, then started reading. Language Arts classes were not his favorite, but he had had some good English teachers, plus at night when he couldn't sleep, he read Tom Clancy and Stephen King novels, and other books, too, though he didn't make a big deal about this with his friends. He didn't want to be called a "booker," like some of the National Honor Society boys in high school.

"Okay, fine," Laura said after only a paragraph. "That word *glaciation*—what does it mean?"

"The root word would be *glacier*," Trace said. "So *glaciation* would be, like, the effects of glaciers?"

"And *geothermal*?" Laura asked.

"Heat from the ground. Probably hot water, like in Yellowstone Park. That sort of thing," he added with a shrug, as if he were in school. "That sort of thing" and the shrug was the standard reply from boys who didn't want to seem overly smart.

"So let's just talk," Laura said, leaning back to put him at ease.

And they did. About school, his career plans (undecided), his family, girlfriends. As Trace blushed, a camera snapped several times; he looked quickly toward the sound. The photographer introduced himself as Carlos.

"Get used to him, dear," Laura said. "If you end up as Team Blu's driver, cameras are going to be a part of your life."

After a few minutes of talk, Laura checked her watch. "Okay, Trace. We're going to waive the writing part—the dreaded paragraph—as your high school transcript says you do well enough in your English classes. Right now, Carlos is going to shoot some more pictures of you in the back while I make some notes, all right?"

Trace nodded. Swallowing, he followed Carlos. A tall stool sat before a silvery backdrop screen. Lights on tripods stood ready.

"Here by the stool—just stand for now," Carlos said. He stepped close to fuss with Trace's collar. Carlos had on some kind of sweet cologne.

"Okay. You look great, Trace. Really. Cross your arms, look straight at me. Chin up a little bit—you've got a great jawline. Just like that! Great!" Carlos said as he clicked away.

Trace followed instructions: sit on the stool, look left, look right.

"Now stand up," Carlos said.

Trace stood up.

"There's that thing drivers do, in hot weather, with their racing suits," Carlos said, as he changed cameras, "where they tie their sleeves around their waist? Let's get one of those."

"Um, I don't have a shirt on underneath," Trace said.

"Don't worry," Carlos said with a high-pitched laugh. "We're not going to post these on the Internet."

Trace did not smile. Reluctantly he unzipped his suit and tied the sleeves across his belly. Laura paused in her scribbling to watch. Trace worked out. He was in good shape, plus he had a vee of dark hair between his pecs. But in the bright lights he felt skinny, pale, and naked.

"Great, thanks," Carlos said.

Trace quickly zipped up his suit.

"One last shot," Carlos said. "Could you turn around please?"

"Which way?" Trace asked.

"Face the screen," Carlos said. "I need one shot from the rear."

"The rear?" Trace said. His jaw tightened with anger.

"Carlos needs all the angles," Laura called from across the motor home. "We need photos of you from all sides."

Trace reluctantly turned to face the blank silver screen.

After that, and not a second too soon, Trace was done.

Outside the trailer, his father was waiting. "How'd it go?" he quickly asked.

Trace looked at him.

"Not good?" his dad asked.

"It went fine," Trace said, turning away, putting distance between himself and the motor home.

His father walked briskly to keep up. "Did something happen in there?"

"Nothing happened."

His father was silent. Then he said, "Well, a job interview is nobody's idea of a good time."

"That's for sure."

Trace calmed down some, but he was still angry. This whole Team Blu thing was screwy in a way he couldn't explain.

"Did they say anything about notifying you? About when they'll make a decision?"

"No," Trace said.

"I guess we're done for the day, then," his father said.

"I am, I know that," Trace muttered.

His father scratched his head. "You want a hot dog? A soda? There's free food."

"We can eat on the way," Trace said, heading to the Chevy. He figured his fan club would see him leaving and get the message that it was time to go home.

3

On Saturday, it was back to good old Headwaters Speedway. No interview, no vocabulary test, no photo shoot, and no father—he was away on "business," code for Linda.

Trace's yellow Street Stock swayed on the trailer behind. Patrick Fletcher rode shotgun in Trace's Ford pickup. Mel had asked Trace if he'd "mind" if Patrick rode along. As if he could say no to her.

"So what do you do in the pits from three o'clock until hot laps?" Patrick asked. He had on clean jeans, plus cowboy boots, newly shined; however, he wore his Cal Hopkins Green 42 black T-shirt and a suitably faded Minnesota Twins cap.

Trace shrugged. "Lots of stuff with the car. Tweaking

the air pressure, grinding the tires, checking the fuel. You'll see guys dropping transmissions and changing rear ends in the pits, but they should have done that at home. The car should be ready to go when you arrive. But I like to get there early and relax. If I show up right before hot laps and jump in the car, I never feel right on the track."

Patrick nodded.

"Sort of like hunting," Trace said. "You have to be in the woods awhile before you deserve to shoot something."

"I don't hunt," Patrick said.

Trace knew that, and drove on in silence. There was something about Patrick that was bringing out a mean streak in Trace—probably because Mel liked him. Just how much, he was never quite sure.

Behind the trailer was Tyler Skarnes in his Chevy truck, complete with gun rack inside and a "United We Stand" bumper sticker. Tyler worked for Don Bonham, and got paid extra for helping with Trace's yellow No. 32. Married with two kids, Tyler seemed way older than twenty-five. Trace's dad, away on his "business," would try to get back in time for the feature.

"Any word from Team Blu?" Patrick asked.

"No," Trace said. They again drove along in silence. "That whole deal was a little strange."

"It was a fun trip," Patrick replied.

"I'm sure it was—for you," Trace said.

Patrick turned to Trace. "Hey, Mel and I are just friends. She asked me if I wanted to ride along."

Trace was silent. Then he said, "Sorry. Not a big deal." He looked down the road as he drove. "It's just that that whole day felt a little weird to me." He kept trying to find the right words for it.

"Felt weird? How so?" Patrick asked.

Trace glanced at him. Patrick waited, eyes wide open, sincere about wanting to know. Tyler and Trace's other motor head friends would never ask a question like that.

"Just . . . lame, that's all," Trace said with a surge of annoyance. Headwaters Speedway came in sight beyond the trees. The pits were nearly empty, and a few cars were scattered by the grandstand.

Patrick leaned forward. "It feels way different to be on the other side," he said.

"The other side?"

"I mean, to be with a race car team as opposed to mowing the lawn or cleaning the johns," Patrick said.

"Hey, you're moving up in the world."

"Yeah, and with no pay today," Patrick added.

"Gee, what'll Mel do without you?" Trace asked.

Patrick looked sideways at him, then back to the grandstand. "Mel does fine on her own," he said.

"I know what you mean," Trace offered. He turned in to the speedway.

At the pit entrance, Trace stopped to pay, sign in, get his wristband, and draw a number—the old-fashioned way.

"You draw for me," he said to Patrick.

"Me? You sure?"

Rebecca and the girls in the pit shack laughed. "Need some luck tonight, Trace?" one of them teased.

Trace nodded toward Patrick; Rebecca held out the pouch and shook it. Chips rattled.

Patrick closed his eyes, reached in—and pulled out number 4.

"All right!" Trace said, throwing up a high five to Patrick.

"Four is good, right?" Patrick asked.

As they drove through the pits, Trace explained the driver draw—the sequence of numbers, the draw's importance to one's heat placement (inside versus outside rows), and so on. "A good forward slot in the heat race generally means you'll do well. The better you do in the heat, the better position you'll have to start the feature. I should have you draw for me all the time."

Tyler behind, Trace pulled into his usual slot, next to the Harkness family. "Racing addicts and then some," he said to Patrick as they got out. "Gerry, the dad, drives a Super Stock. The kid, Tim, who just turned sixteen, drives a Pure Stock."

"The mother is the crew chief," Tyler added as he walked up. "She knows more about cars than anyone out here."

Cigarette dangling from her mouth, Cindy Harkness looked up from her handheld grinder. Secured on a detachable hub on the side of their car hauler, a tire slowly turned beneath her blue cordless Makita. She nodded at

Trace without changing the rhythm of her grinder's slow passes over the face of the tire. Trace thought of his own mother, Sharon. She was a totally different kind of woman: a financial planner, a runner, a fitness fanatic, a well-dressed businesswoman who liked things neat and tidy at home, and a life where all the numbers added up—which was not the case in either racing or farming.

"What's she doing?" Patrick asked.

"See how the tire is darker where she's ground it?" Trace said. "She's roughing up the surface."

"Why?"

"More fresh rubber means better traction. Especially in dry slick conditions."

"What's 'dry slick'?" Patrick asked.

Trace stared for a moment; it was going to be a long night. "That's when the track dries out, and gets hard and shiny—and slippery."

"Great bus," Patrick said, casting his gaze to the Harkness family's rig.

Some people hauled race cars with pickups, others with motor homes, still others with expensive tractor-trailer units. The Harkness family used an old yellow school bus. Just behind the cab were living quarters, complete with curtained windows and hillbilly air conditioner—a window unit that poked out, its cord running back to a small Honda generator. The generator, toolbox, and tire rack fronted the last thirty or so feet of the bus, which had been sheared off and made into a flatbed hauler for their race cars.

"Hey, kid," Gerry Harkness called to Trace.

"Hey, boss," Trace replied. It was their standard greeting.

Gerry ambled over. As did his wife, Gerry smoked like a woodstove in a Minnesota winter. "So how'd that tryout go in Grand Forks?" he asked.

Trace knew that he knew, but didn't mind the question. "Lousy," he said. "Missed my spots in the turns. Too much brake, not enough throttle. Just wasn't smooth."

"Hey, you got your shot anyway," Gerry said, letting out a sigh as if this was the luck of all who raced at Headwaters.

"He wasn't totally lousy," Patrick said.

Gerry glanced at Patrick.

"You should have seen some of those kids," Tyler added as he started to loosen the come-along. "It was like they'd been driving Super Stocks since kindergarten."

"So what was that whole Team Blu thing?" Gerry asked Trace. Cindy stopped grinding to listen.

"To be honest, I don't know," Trace said; he knelt to help Tyler pull back the chains that held down the Street Stock.

"Well, I started from scratch and worked my way up," Gerry said, glancing over at his battered cars and school-bus hauler. "No reason you can't, too."

"Right," Trace said, with a glance to Patrick.

"Say, when you get a chance, can you listen to Tim's engine?" Gerry asked. "It don't sound right."

"Sure," Trace said. "Let's do it now."

"He's always up for engine stuff," said Tyler. "Gets him out of any real work."

As Patrick and Tyler unloaded the car, Trace headed over to Tim's beat-up Monte Carlo. They unpinned the hood, lifted it free.

"Fire it up," Trace said to Tim, a stubby kid in a hand-me-down black racing suit.

As Tim sat in the car, Trace leaned over the vibrating, throbbing engine and worked the throttle linkage back and forth.

"Enough," Trace called to Tim, who killed the engine.

"What d'ya think?" Gerry asked.

"It's running rich," Trace said.

"Told you," Cindy said as she continued grinding. Gerry ignored her.

"Let's pop out a spark plug to make sure," Trace said.

Tim found a wrench and socket; Trace backed out the number one plug. He held it up to the daylight—looked closely at its tip, its gap, its threads. "You got baby bear syndrome," Trace said. "It's black and furry."

"Those are nearly new plugs!" Gerry said.

Trace rolled the spark plug in his fingers to check the brand. "Where'd you get these?"

Gerry coughed, and glanced across the track. "The hardware store."

"Gerry, you're not driving a lawn mower," Trace said. "Spend some money on a decent set of plugs!"

"Told you," Cindy said to her husband.

By five o'clock the pits were filling with race cars, each team parking in its usual spot. The Bialacheks from up near Hibbing on the Iron Range rumbled in with their long, old-school tractor-trailer rig and the No. 28 Super Stock. Their spot was trackside, just beyond the pit bleachers. The crew always erected a collapsible metal safety railing around the trailer's roof—there was ladder access from inside—then set up lawn chairs for viewing the racetrack. There were always some hot girls hanging out up there, but they never came down and mingled.

A local new guy at the track, Bill Showalter, rolled in. He was in real estate and financial services, and had gotten a bad bug for racing. He went out and bought the biggest car hauler at the track: a Freightliner tractor with a forty-eight-foot trailer that had a full shop inside. But his crew was right out of *The Simpsons*, two guys who never seemed to know what they were doing. It was scary just watching them unload the race car. Someday one of them was going to run over the other.

Trace pointed out the other regulars: Amber Jenkins and her Mod-Four and crew of brothers. Beau Kim, another Mod-Four racer, was rebuilding, but never missed a Saturday night in the pits. There was Mindy, twenty-one, and her pink Mini-Stock, touched up every week by a doting dad; on hot nights in the pits, she wore her racing suit tied sleeves across the waist and a little white, bare-shouldered T-shirt. Along with Mindy was a new girl from the Red Lake Indian Reservation who drove a dark red Mini-Stock. Girl cars were easy to spot; they usually carried something cute—a little bear or a monkey or a dreamcatcher—tied to the interior roll cage.

"You should get a Mini-Stock," Tyler said to Patrick. He glanced sideways at Trace, expecting him to be amused—the whole girl-car thing.

"Yeah, right," Patrick said.

Trace stared at Patrick. "Hey, why not?" he said. "They're cheap. Plus the speedway always needs new cars and drivers. The problem with small-town tracks like this one is that the same people in the same cars place generally in the same order every night."

"My parents would kill me!" Patrick said.

"You don't know that," Trace said.

Patrick was silent; he looked at the race cars again.

Across the track, fans began to spatter themselves across the grandstand bleachers. Trace pointed out the fat lady in her usual spot, high up on the left side; she never missed a race, and always had a large green umbrella for shade or rain. Below, at track level, the water truck rumbled past in low gear, its horizontal pipe throwing even needles of water onto the brown clay mix. Everything was in its place—which was when Trace's phone vibrated.

VISITORS 2 C U. It was Mel.

WHO? Trace keyed back.

ON THEIR WAY, Mel answered.

4

"What?" Patrick asked as Trace shut his phone.

"I'm not sure what," Trace said. He looked down pit row. Then he saw them, two dark figures picking their way along between the cars and mud puddles: Carlos and Tasha.

"Gotta be kidding," Trace muttered.

Patrick followed his gaze. "Hey, they're from—"

"Team Blu," Trace finished.

Patrick looked at him. "You know what this means?" His voice rose with excitement.

"Stay cool. Don't do anything stupid," Trace said. His stomach flip-flopped.

One by one the local pit crews stopped to watch Carlos and Tasha pass. It was as if someone had pressed a

giant pause button: air wrenches ceased their rattle, ciga-
rettes stopped halfway to mouths, tire grinders polished
air. Then each crew member resumed work, but with a
long look over the shoulder.

Tasha spotted Trace, and waved.

"So great to see you again, Trace!" Carlos said, hurrying
forward to give Trace a big hug. He wore orange foam
earplugs that stuck out like little tumors.

"Uh, yeah, you too—" Trace said, trying to extricate
himself. Next to them, the Harkness family cacophony of
grinding, hammering, and arguing had gone silent.

"Hey, Trace," Tasha said, her dark eyes full of amuse-
ment. She gave him a strong handshake, but no hug (not
that he would have minded).

"So what brings you guys here?" Trace asked, surprised
to have found any words. But this was his home turf; he
was comfortable here.

Tasha glanced at Patrick and Tyler.

"It's okay. They're with me," Trace said.

She lowered her voice. "Laura Williams could not be
here to tell you in person, but she is pleased to inform you
that you're a finalist for the Team Blu ride."

"Congratulations!" Carlos added.

Trace shifted his feet to a wider stance; he suddenly
needed more balance, as if the ground was tilting.

"A finalist? Among how many?" Patrick asked.

"Three," Tasha said quietly to Trace. "Right now we're
visiting each of the finalists at his or her home speedway
to get a few more photos. If that's all right?"

Trace was silent. *His or her.* That meant Sara from Fargo was still in the mix. Maybe.

Patrick nudged him.

"Uh, sure, fire away," Trace said.

Just then the chief pit steward from WISSOTA came putt-putting along on his ATV, wearing his usual fluorescent green safety vest and radio headphones. "Packing!" he called to Trace, and then again to the Harkness family.

Gerry Harkness swore without heat and flipped a one-finger salute at the departing official. Everybody hated packing.

"Sorry, gotta go," Trace said to Carlos and Tasha. "Every driver has to help pack the track before the races. We don't have a sheepsfoot or a regular packer, so the cars have to do it."

As Trace zipped up his suit and got into his car, Carlos snapped away with his camera. Inside the car, Trace fired the engine and briefly hammered the accelerator. Carlos flinched and backed off, which was a good thing; Trace didn't want to run him over. As he rumbled off down pit row, Trace glanced back to see Patrick gesturing to the empty folding chairs on the trailer, and talking easily with Tasha. It was good to have a guy around with some social skills.

The track was as muddy as a low spot in a cornfield after a cloudburst. George, the track's dirt man, had recently been out with the rickety watering truck sprinkling the track. Northern Minnesota had plenty of water, and George was not shy about using it. As Trace crawled around the track with the other Street and Pure Stocks, clots of wet clay slapped and spattered. On the banked turns, Trace's rear wheels threatened to break loose and slip downward—he had to accelerate briefly to keep a straight line. One Pure Stock, moving too slowly, slid butt-backward down to the edge of the infield. But gradually the steady line of tires pressed the moisture deeper into the dirt, and the flagman waved the Street and Pure Stocks off the track and the lighter Mini-Stocks and Mod-Fours on for their share of mud work.

Heading back into the pits, Trace's Street Stock felt like a tractor at a tractor pull. There was probably a hundred pounds of wet clay stuck to his undercarriage. His water temperature was up, too; the front-end rock guard, a square of wire mesh over his radiator, had mudded shut. A radiator needs airflow to breathe, to let off heat. Approaching his pit slot, Trace blipped the accelerator several times and gestured at Tyler—who brought around the water can. Nearly all race teams had one, an old-fashioned fire extinguisher, the silvery, five-gallon-canister kind with a short spray hose on top. Water under air pressure (also good for post-race water fights between pit crews) is perfect for cutting mud. Tyler sprayed the nose of the Street Stock even as Trace braked to a stop.

Trace remained in the cockpit, watching his heat gauge, keeping the engine running at a couple thousand rpm. As Tyler put up a brown mist of muddy water, the needle gradually dropped to 180 degrees, then 160 and downward. The key thing was never to shut off a hot engine, but to get the heat down first.

"We're good!" Trace called, and killed the engine. He swung out through the window—to the *clickety-click* of Carlos's camera.

"Great! Excellent!" the photographer said, as Trace took off his mud-spattered helmet and set it on the roof. Carlos took a couple of close-up shots of it.

"Now comes the fun part," Trace said. He handed out several skinny mini-shovels—like ice scrapers but with longer handles and wider plastic paddles.

"What's this?" Tasha asked, looking at hers.

"For the mud," Trace said, with a nod to his car.

"I get it," Tasha replied, and set to work. Carlos snapped away as Trace's crew—and Tasha—de-mudded his car.

"Good grief, there's a lot of it!" Tasha said, poking her scraper under the wheel well. Shiny brown clumps piled up on the ground.

The pit boss zoomed past on his ATV. "Pit meeting. All drivers. Pit meeting!"

"Can we come?" Carlos asked.

Trace headed with his entourage of Patrick, Tasha, and Carlos to the pit shack area. Gradually the drivers, all wearing racing suits, most tied at the waist, gathered. Some drivers wore no shirts underneath (it was eighty-five degrees and humid). There were lots of bad tattoos and some seriously hairy backs. Carlos fired away. Trace kept his suit on and fully zipped.

"Welcome to Headwaters Speedway," the chief pit steward began. He stood on the back of his ATV and read from well-worn notes.

Trace knew the whole speech—it was like a flight attendant's instructions on seat belts and exits—but it was useful information for out-of-town drivers: where to come on and off the track, penalties (two places) for jumping the gun on a green flag, rules for restarts, rules for changing a tire on a yellow flag, who had to weigh in and go to the tech lane after the race, et cetera.

"What's the 'tech lane'?" Tasha asked.

"It's the place where the officials inspect your car after the race to make sure you're not cheating," Trace answered. "The top five finishers in each class usually get teched."

The pit boss continued. "Some of you didn't pack tonight—numbers 40 and 22 in Modifieds, and 86 and 27 in Super Stock—which means you start in the rear."

There were some jeers, especially from Gerry Harkness. As with most drivers, he had no love for the pit boss—it was a cat-and-dog kind of thing.

"Also, check your weight jacks if you're using them. Last week over in Grand Rapids, somebody's weight came off. Six inches closer and it would have killed a Modified driver. As is, it took out two of his window bars."

The drivers fell silent.

"Weight jacks?" Tasha whispered.

"Pieces of lead bolted to the rear frame. It's all about getting the right weight in the right spot for the best traction," Trace said.

"Your weights *must* have your car's number stamped or

painted on them," the pit boss continued. "It's in the rule book. That way, when I find somebody's weight on the track, I can disqualify them for the season."

A wave of muttering passed among the drivers, but nobody disagreed.

"He's certainly a crabby guy!" Carlos observed—in a moment of dead airspace.

The pit boss turned his sunglasses to Carlos and gave him a long look; all the drivers laughed. Carlos ducked behind Trace, and the pit boss continued. When he'd wrapped it up, the drivers lingered for small talk; it was the only time they were all together, and a good opportunity for them to needle one another.

"You're actually considering this pip-squeak as a driver?" Gerry said to Tasha and Carlos. Clearly everybody knew about Team Blu.

"We're giving him a look," Tasha said easily.

Gerry wrapped Trace in a friendly headlock. "You'd be better off making him crew chief. He knows a lot about engines, but he's lousy behind the wheel." Gerry gave Trace a brisk knuckle rub as the other drivers hooted.

Conrad Moe, another Street Stock driver, added, "We like Trace so much we're gonna make sure he runs last tonight—right, boys?"

This brought more laughter as Trace struggled to extricate himself from Gerry's big, deodorant-free armpit.

"Everybody seems to get along great," Tasha said as they headed back to Trace's slot.

"Off the track, yes," Trace said. "On the track—well, that's a different thing."

In his heat, Trace started in the pole position—first row, inside. But the pole slot was overrated; drivers directly behind learned from the leader's mistakes. Watching the pole car was a lesson in what the track conditions would give, and smart drivers always took advantage. As well, starting on the inside gave him fewer places to go—so Trace powered up hard at the green flag. Get out front and stay out front—that was the plan.

Which was his first mistake. Trace led the pack through turn 1, but pushed way too hard and high into turn 2. Suddenly he found himself in traffic heading down the straightaway—resulting in a three-wide plunge into turn 3. Nobody gave an inch, and Trace's Street Stock got pinched like a walnut in a nutcracker. Sheet metal shrieked as all three cars went briefly sideways. Trace fought the wheel, and had no option but to brake hard. The other two, including Conrad, surged past; Trace fell in behind them. Something was flapping and banging on his left rear side, and by lap 4 he felt a sudden shudder in his steering wheel: flat tire.

He swore, and looked for a slot in the dust in order to exit through turn 3.

Tyler and Patrick waited as Trace pulled to a stop. He hoisted himself out of the car.

Carlos looked puzzled. "Aren't you guys supposed to

swarm over the car and change his tire?" he said to Trace's crew.

"You've been watching too much NASCAR," Tyler said. "This is small-town Minnesota, not Talladega."

"What happens now with the feature race?" Tasha asked, her eye going to the flat tire.

"I start in the back," Trace answered.

"We call that 'passing practice,' " Gerry Harkness added. "Lord knows he needs it."

Trace sat with Tasha and Patrick in the pit bleachers to watch the rest of the heat races. He answered all their questions about flags, protocols, restarts, car classes, and so on.

Tasha took a long look behind them at the families, the crews, the race cars. "It's definitely not Talladega," she said, "but you could get there from here, right?"

Trace followed her gaze across the pits and the home-made car haulers, the rough-and-ready teams, the beat-up cars. "Conceivably," he said. "It could happen."

"That's what you drivers dream about, right?" Tasha asked.

In a feature race, sometimes it paid to start at the rear. Up front, in turn 1, the leading Street Stocks banged and rocked one another like wild horses whipped through a narrow canyon. Staying high and to the outside, Trace avoided contact, and picked up at least four places. Gobs of mud flew, and slapped his helmet visor like giant brown beetles exploding against a windshield. Trace yanked a visor tear-off tab in order to clear his vision; the narrow strip of cellophane fluttered away behind. Depending upon track conditions, he would tear away several during a race.

On lap 2, the same drivers tried the same maneuver in the same turn—sending two cars over the rim and off the track in an explosion of dust. Yellow flag! On the single-file restart, Trace found himself ninth of fourteen cars. Passing the pit bleachers at caution speed, he saw his crew waving encouragement. Tasha was clapping; Carlos's camera covered his face. Ahead, the corner man waggled his closed yellow flag toward the orange starting cone. Green flag coming!

Conrad Moe, leading the pack in his red and white No. 12, held the pace to a growling crawl. He kept them slow and deep into turn 3—then powered up at the apex of the turn. Race cars at the green flag were like regular cars at traffic light: they all took off. But unlike in street driving, when cars started forward one at a time—consecutively—on the racetrack cars surged all at once. This took a lot of faith that none of the drivers would brake or lose nerve. It was also the part Trace liked about racing. Everyone on the track usually knew what they were doing, and drove accordingly. This made racing actually safer than driving in regular freeway traffic.

But stock car drivers are not immune to stupid moves. In turn 4, blue No. 24, driven by Josh Greenway, tried a high-low dive, which left him quartering sideways through the apex—and vulnerable to the slightest contact. In tight traffic this was inevitable. Red and yellow No. 61 nudged Greenway's left rear quarter-panel and sent No. 24 into a whipping, 360-degree spin. Traffic broke to both sides of Greenway, who ended up backward and stalled in the infield. Another yellow flag. Trace took the opportunity to pull away another tear-off, and shake some sticky clay from his racing gloves.

For the restart, the Street Stocks stopped, single-file, as the spotters and flagmen figured out the order. On bigger, more modern tracks, each car carried a transponder, and a computer kept continuous track of the cars. By rights, whoever caused the yellow flag went to the rear. Trace, sitting somewhere around eighth position, waited for the call. He was surprised to see Greenway's No. 24 waved forward into the fourth position. No. 61 surged up alongside Trace, and its driver gestured angrily at the pit steward in the lime-green safety vest.

"Not my fault the moron can't drive!" the driver shouted (Trace read his lips).

The chief steward shrugged, tapped his earphones, pointed to the grandstand booth where such calls were made, and waved No. 61 "tailback," or to the rear.

Trace moved up to seventh.

On the third restart, he timed the green perfectly, and streamed past two cars up high. He worried that he was too high, but had enough slingshot momentum to try his own dive. Knifing perfectly downward between two cars—more luck than skill—he came out side by side on the low line with the third-place car, No. 24. Greenway looked surprised.

They went like magnets stuck to each other into the next turn, with Trace pushing Greenway high and onto the marbles. Greenway lost traction, and Trace pulled away.

"Okay, baby!" he shouted to his Street Stock. Second place with five laps to go.

The lead car, Conrad's No. 12, was five or six lengths ahead, and Trace concentrated on being smooth through the turns. Drivers who made the turns look exciting were not driving smart or driving well. The goal in the turns was to look boring—which meant smooth. Gradually, Trace began to reel Conrad in. He jerked away another tear-off (three left); he wanted clear vision for the last few laps.

With three laps to go, he was on Conrad's bumper.

At two laps to go, Trace laid his Street Stock's nose along Conrad's driver's door. Conrad, an experienced driver, did not look at Trace; instead, he tried to pinch off Trace's line.

Second place was a lock, but on the final lap Conrad missed his spot in turn 3. He drove too deep into the turn, and had to take a higher line—and the higher the line, the longer the track. Trace gambled by braking and going lower. It cost him momentum, but it also shortened his distance to the checkered flag.

Both drivers powered up at the same moment, but by then Trace was half a car length ahead. With his engine roaring full tilt, Trace thundered beneath the checkered flag an arm's length ahead of Conrad.

"Yes!" he shouted, and pumped his fist. As he came past the pit bleachers, Tasha and his crew jumped up and down and clapped.

Trace turned sharply into the infield for his weigh-in. Then it was on to victory lane, the black-and-white checkerboard of concrete directly across the grandstand. Billboards of local sponsors formed the backdrop. Trace swung himself out of the car to applause from the grandstand. He waved to the crowd, then waited as the trophy kid came across the track, hand in hand with his dad. Chosen by an earlier drawing, trophy kids got to meet the winning drivers and receive little trophies of their own.

As the local newspaper photographer, Dennis Anderson, arranged the kid, the flag, the trophy, and Trace, Carlos rushed up panting.

"He's with me," Trace said quickly to Dennis.

Carlos began to snap away as Trace knelt in the late sunlight with the little boy and their trophies.

Back in the pits, Trace arrived to a happy crew. Gerry Harkness came over to wrap him in a big, sweaty hug. "You done good, kid."

Trace posed for a few more photos, then slugged down a full bottle of water as Carlos snapped away.

"Enough, man!" Trace said.

"Never enough," Carlos said. "It's what I do."

Afterward, Trace took Carlos and Tasha over to the grandstand to watch the rest of the features. In the stands, Trace shook and slapped hands with friends and neighbors.

Even Mel came out of the booth. "Nice race," she said, giving him a hug and an actual peck on the cheek.

"Whoa!" Trace said. He held her an extra moment; she didn't seem to mind. Of course Carlos got the photo.

"Hi there," Tasha said to Mel.

"Sorry," Trace said quickly, releasing Mel and making the introductions. Mel shook hands. She was wearing sunglasses, which made it difficult to gauge her expression— but she wasn't smiling.

"Hope Headwaters Speedway is not too small for you," Mel said.

"Not at all," Tasha said easily.

"I love it here!" Carlos said, looking around the stands. "It's so rustic. Most of these people could be in the movies—as extras, I mean."

"Except for Trace, who's a star now, right?" Mel said, with a look at Tasha.

As Mel headed back to the booth, Tasha looked at Trace. "What was that all about?"

"I'm not sure," Trace said. His gaze followed Mel. The announcer's booth door slammed behind her hard enough to rattle the glass.

"Oh, I get it!" Tasha said, and smiled.

"No, that's not it," Trace said quickly.

"But you sorta wish it was, right?" Tasha teased.

Trace shrugged and held back the smallest of grins. They all sat down to watch the next race. As the Mod-Fours came whining onto the track for their feature, Tasha leaned close to Trace. "You should know," she said, the engine noise a perfect muffler to her voice, "that this Team Blu ride is pretty much yours."

Trace turned to her.

"If you want it, that is," she added.

5

Yellow dust—finely chopped straw, not racetrack dirt—sprayed his windshield. It was Thursday, and Trace steered his day-cab Kenworth grain hauler alongside a tall, humming combine. It was harvesttime in northwestern Minnesota, and Trace made good money running wheat from field to elevator. Usually there was a "runner," a tractor pulling a grain cart, that brought the wheat to the truck, but the grain-cart guy was busy in the next field. Trace had orders to load directly from the combine—on the fly.

Combine drivers were obsessed with not stopping, because they got paid by the acre. As Trace came alongside, the driver signaled for him to move up, then turned back to watch his cockpit readouts. Rolling side by side, Trace eased a half-length ahead, positioning his trailer under the combine's outstretched auger. He kept careful pace with the roaring, dusty green elephant in his right side mirror. The combine's auger chattered briefly, then quieted. A leg-thick stream of wheat poured into the rear of Trace's hauler; he couldn't see it, but soon felt the gathering weight.

In the middle of this, his phone rattled.

Steering with one arm, Trace answered without checking the number. "Yeah?"

"This is Laura Williams from Team Blu."

He froze. Time stopped. Literally. Suddenly the combine driver was looking down and jerking his finger angrily for Trace to move up.

"Listen, I'm driving a truck, I can't talk right now!" Trace said, bringing up his rpm and watching his mirror.

"Sure you can," Laura replied briskly.

"No, really, I can't. Give me five minutes," Trace said. He clapped shut his phone.

In the field behind his truck lay a pile of wheat like a yellow snowdrift, fifty bushels at least. Wild geese would be happy for the spilled grain, but the combine driver was another matter. Trace made sure to keep a steady, parallel pace. Soon enough the auger chattered again—the combine's hopper was empty. The driver waved him off, mouthing a few choice words at Trace as he moved away through the spray of straw. When Trace's windshield had cleared, he made a slow, wide turn back to the field exit; no matter how dry and firm the field, he knew how easily he could get stuck if he stopped a loaded truck on wheat stubble.

Back on the hard gravel of the township road, he powered down the big Cummins diesel, set the air brakes— and returned Laura's call.

"Don't ever do that to me again," she said.

No hello. No nothing. "Sorry," Trace said. "I was in the middle of a work thing and—"

"Team Blu is a bigger thing, all right?" she replied.

Trace was silent.

"You still there?" Laura asked.

"You broke up for a second," Trace lied.

"Anyway," Laura said, her tone lightening a half note, "I have good news. Our Team Blu members, along with our ad agency people in Minneapolis, have unanimously chosen you to be our Super Stock driver."

Trace's brain went blank.

"Did I break up again?"

"Wow," Trace said.

Laura actually laughed. Briefly. "I thought you might say something like that," she replied. "Anyway, things are moving quickly. We need you in Minneapolis tomorrow morning to meet the rest of the team, including Mr. Rupert, the CEO, though he'll be in New York, but we'll do a videoconference with him and—"

"Wait, wait, wait!" Trace said.

"What?"

"I can't be in Minneapolis tomorrow."

"Why not?"

"I have a job—"

"That truck-driving thing?"

"Yes."

"Quit," Laura said. "There are other people around. Anyone can drive a truck."

"Yeah, but—"

"But Minneapolis is five hours away," she said, mimicking his voice and tone.

"That's true," Trace said.

"Don't worry about that. We're sending a plane for you."

Trace paused.

"Trace?"

"Yes. Still here."

"You have an airport, our company has a plane. What time can you be ready to go in the morning? Tasha says you should be at your airport no later than eight a.m."

"Eight a.m.?" Trace replied.

"Yes. You do want this job, right?"

After he shut his phone, Trace was silent. Then he opened the door and dropped through humid air onto hard ground. Far off, combines moved under small, pale domes of dust. Grain-hauler trucks waited in the wings. There were no cars, no people, only a flock of geese moving slow and low. He took a pee, then leaned against the hot, dusty side of the trailer to suck in some long, deep breaths.

The next morning, Trace waited at the Headwaters Airport with his dad. It was agreed, in a couple of follow-up calls, that a "parent or guardian" should be with him. His father was clean-shaven, lively, and excited. Trace was mostly silent. Across the parking lot was the regular passenger terminal, a newer building where the Northwest Airlines Mesaba Airlink planes came and went. But Trace was to be picked up at the private plane terminal next door. Small plane owners, local pilots, and crop-sprayer guys came and went through the open doors.

"Here comes your bird," said the desk manager, Dave, a cheerful, round-faced guy; he glanced toward the runway.

A narrow white twin-engine prop plane came in fast and smooth. As its tires touched down in a silent puff of blue smoke, the grasshoppers in Trace's stomach lifted off.

"Cheyenne turboprop," Dave said. "Nice plane. You'll be in the Twin Cities in fifty minutes."

Trace and his dad stood up.

"When it comes to a complete stop, just head through the door there, and climb aboard." Dave nodded sideways to the simple metal door.

"Ready?" Trace's dad asked him.

"I guess," Trace said.

When the props stopped turning, they went through the door, no security required.

They approached the plane. Close up, its props and

fuselage were bigger than Trace had expected. The pilot, bent over, writing something, glanced up from the cockpit; he disappeared from view, and soon the side door swung down.

"Trace and Don Bonham?" the pilot said, glancing at his clipboard. He was young but had an all-business face and manner—always reassuring in pilots.

"That's us," Trace's dad said.

"All aboard for Minneapolis," he said.

Trace was silent most of the way. It was only he and his dad in the six seats, along with the pilot and his squawking radio up front. His dad made small talk—about the fields below, the number of central-pivot irrigators. Trace watched the passing landscape: lakes, houses, barns, an oval dirt track on somebody's farm. Tiny cars inched along string-thin highways.

"The flight attendant is me," the pilot called back. "There's soft drinks in that little fridge."

Trace opened a cola. The bubbles felt good in his stomach.

The plane landed at Holman Field near downtown St. Paul. "Way faster in and out for all of us," the pilot said as they taxied up to an old-fashioned terminal. "The Minneapolis Airport is a zoo, plus you gotta go through all that security." He pointed beyond the fence to a black Town Car. "That should be your ride."

The driver, a young guy with red-rimmed eyes and a black sport coat in need of dry cleaning, held open the back door.

"Halloran and Peterson ad agency, IDS building," Trace's father said.

"Got you covered," the driver said without looking fully at them. He was not interested in making conversation, and drove fast through traffic on Freeway 94 west to Minneapolis.

Nicollet Mall was closed to regular traffic, but not to the Lincoln Town Car. Ahead, soaring straight up, the blue-green glass sides of the IDS Tower reflected skyscrapers and puffy white passing clouds.

The driver walked them into the gymnasium-sized court, where water fell from the glass ceiling into a wide, round pond. Tasha was waiting.

"Hey, Trace, Mr. Bonham," she said, shaking hands with Trace's father. "Congrats!" She gave Trace a quick high-five.

"Thanks," Trace managed to say.

"You all right?" Tasha asked.

"Yeah. Sure," Trace said.

The driver left without waiting to be paid. Trace glanced over his shoulder and watched him disappear. So far this trip was in a parallel universe to the way regular people traveled. He followed Tasha to the elevators.

"Chew gum or swallow," she said as the door whispered shut behind them. "This baby will make your ears pop."

They exited on the forty-second floor into a reception area fronting a maze of hallways. A beefy security guard who looked Hawaiian lingered at the high counter, chatting with a secretary. Tall potted plants dotted the corners; large abstract paintings and stainless-steel wall art hung above a cluster of low brown leather couches.

"This way," Tasha said, with a nod to the security guy. She led them past the receiving area and down a richly carpeted and dimly lit hallway.

The offices of Halloran & Peterson jumped with music and action. Hip-looking people, young and artsy, passed among computer desks and poster-size photos of models and products. The carpet was pale gold.

Laura strode forward, hand outstretched to his father, and then to Trace. "Your trip went well?"

"Great," Trace said, still looking around.

"Plane okay? I hope you weren't expecting a Learjet."

"It was fine," Trace said.

"This way, then," Laura said.

Trace followed her into a board-meeting-type room with a long oval table, a big flat-screen and projector system—and a million-dollar view. The skyline of Minneapolis stretched beside and below them. The walls were floor-to-ceiling glass.

"It can be a little scary at first," Tasha said.

Trace took a step closer to the glass, and looked down.

"We even have our own hawks," Laura said from across the room as she arranged some papers.

"Falcons, actually," Tasha said cheerfully. "Peregrine falcons."

"Hawks, falcons, falcons, hawks," Laura replied, not looking up.

"They nest on the ledge—over there—can you see it?" Tasha said, stepping close to Trace. She pointed.

Trace carefully leaned toward the glass. Sure enough, there was the nest, a little heap of sticks and trash knitted together, tucked against a square corner of glass.

"I've read about the falcons," Trace said. "They eat pigeons, right?"

"They sure do," Tasha said. "You don't even want to watch when they bring one back to the nest."

"So is everybody here?" Laura called to Tasha. "Mr. Rupert keyed up?"

"All set," Tasha said. At that moment Carlos bustled in with a laptop.

"We'll look at pictures while we wait," Laura said.

When Carlos had finished setting up, the room lights dimmed and the wall screen glowed purple. Carlos's PowerPoint show began with Rivers Speedway in Grand Forks: the pits, the Super Stock, the assembled drivers, and Cal Hopkins. Then it was Trace in his racing suit beside the car, in the car, out of the car.

"Looking good!" Carlos said.

"We'll be the judge of that," Laura said. Carlos laughed; Laura didn't.

The show moved to shots of Trace in the studio, looking left, looking right; standing up, sitting down.

"Love the profile, the jawline," Laura said to Carlos.

"I told you," Carlos said.

The photos then switched to Headwaters Speedway: the pits, Trace's yellow No. 32 Street Stock, Trace with the checkered flag in the winner's square. He was sweaty, his face shiny and streaked with dust; the little kid smiled up at Trace.

"Carlos, we don't pay you enough," Laura said.

"You're too, too kind!" Carlos said with a giggle. "Please tell Mr. Rupert."

"Yeah, right," Laura said.

Then came a photo of Mel kissing Trace on the cheek.

"Who's that?" Laura asked.

"Mel—Melody—Walters," Trace said. "She manages the speedway."

"Your girlfriend?" Laura asked.

"No," Trace fumbled.

"I kinda think so, myself," Tasha said.

Laura turned to Trace. "She's pretty. We should get some pix of you and her." Then she gestured for Carlos to kill the slide show. "Anyway," she said, turning to Trace. "We all liked your look. You were our unanimous choice."

"My look and my driving?" Trace asked.

His father looked surprised.

"Of course," Laura replied quickly, with a trace of annoyance. "You're a solid driver. We think you're the full package."

"I've always thought so, too," Don said, trying for a joke. "He's a good kid."

Laura stared a moment at Don. "I have to ask you a question," she said. "Business for us, personal for you, but we'd like to know."

"Shoot," Don said.

"Your wife? Trace's mom?"

Don's eyes narrowed.

"It's my understanding she doesn't live with you?" Laura asked.

"That's right," Don said.

Trace glanced out the window.

"She hasn't been part of the family for about two years now," Don said.

"Are you divorced?" Laura asked bluntly.

"No. It's in progress, but moving slowly."

"So you share custody of Trace?"

"That's right. Sharon lives in Eau Claire."

"What does she do? Her job."

"She's a financial planner. She got an offer to move up, to the regional office."

"And she took it," Laura said.

There was a moment of dead airspace in the room.

"It's a bit more than that, but yes, she took it," Trace's dad said.

Laura made some notes. "When we get to the business end, there are some liability release forms involving Trace as a minor. Do you anticipate any problem with her signing off on these?"

Trace let his gaze swing sideways to his father. Their eyes met.

Don hesitated. "No," he said.

Laura made a note, then nodded to Carlos. "Okay. So let's get to the fun stuff."

The lights dimmed slightly as another slide appeared:

the interior of a speed shop. Clamped to a jig, like a streamlined iron sculpture in an art gallery, was the bare pipe frame of a Super Stock. Two guys, hoods down, knelt on the floor as they welded tube joints. The walls of the shop were hung with racks of metal tubing, axles, front-end clips, coil springs, and more—anything needed to build a race car from the ground up. Leaning against the near wall was a stack of bright blue sheet metal.

"This is the Peabody chassis shop in Tennessee," Laura said. "We have contracted with them to build our Team Blu car and provide a crew."

Trace glanced at his father.

"If you don't mind my asking, why not do that here in the Midwest?" Don said.

"Our research shows more dirt track racing, more tracks, more car builders, more expertise the farther south you go," Laura said.

"Sure," Don said. "Stock car racing is stronger in the South. That's where it all started. But there are plenty of shops up here in the Midwest that could build a car and—"

"We're a business," Laura said brusquely. "We make decisions for particular reasons. If the depth of racing tradition is stronger farther south, we'll import that expert-ise north. And by doing that, we offset the variable of having a rookie driver."

Don and Trace were silent.

"You mean, we win races by having better equipment?" Trace asked.

"Something like that," Laura replied, with a glance sideways to Tasha. "We'll need to win, but winning all the time is not the sole objective of Team Blu. If it was, Mr. Rupert would not be involved. He's smarter than that."

Don glanced at Trace.

"Next," Laura said to Carlos.

More slides showed the tinwork—blue panels going onto the sides, then around the cockpit to form the flat deck nose to tail. Then an engine, bright orange block and shiny chrome valve covers, hanging above the empty compartment; then the engine in place, with its round air cleaner poking through the hood.

Trace wanted to ask about the engine—who built it, at what shop, what compression, what dyno results—but he kept quiet.

Then came slides of the complete car, fiberglass nose and facsimile headlights in place, but no lettering, decals, or number: only a shiny, bright blue, fast-looking Super Stock.

"The car should have been done and here for the time trials," Laura said, the corners of her red lipstick turning down ever so slightly. "But there was some delay with the engine builder. However, we're still on schedule for our product launch."

"Which we need to ask about," Trace's dad said.

"Of course," Laura answered. She waited.

"What . . . is it?" Don asked. "Your product?"

"There's really no mystery," Laura said. "Team Blu is a division of Karchers and Ladwin, a worldwide privately owned agribusiness corporation. We are gearing up to launch an energy drink marketed to twelve- to eighteen-year-olds."

"Like Red Bull?" Trace asked.

Laura actually smiled. "There you go," she said. "Our market research people think there's plenty of room for another brand of energy drink. Market segmentation numbers show that teenagers will drink Blu just as readily as Red Bull. They're not brand-loyal. They just want the boost."

"So Trace would be some kind of spokesperson for your drink?" Don asked.

"Oh, heavens no," Laura said. "Real actors will do our commercials. Trace and his car will be—how to put this?—the central image. The car, Trace, and the whole racing thing all tie together for good, old-fashioned niche marketing: teenagers who love auto racing."

"And our logline is *so* brilliant!" Carlos began.

"But strictly under wraps for now," Laura said quickly.

"What's a logline?" Trace asked.

"It's that catchy, one-sentence line that summarizes your product," Laura said. "Movie ads use them, and so do we. Any more questions?" She checked her wristwatch.

Trace was silent for a moment. Then he said, "Yeah. Lots."

"Good," Laura said. "We'll get to all of them. Just be assured that we're not selling tobacco or liquor products, or a restaurant chain with server girls in tights and skimpy T-shirts."

"Counting down," Tasha said. "We're poised to go live with Mr. Rupert."

On the big screen, an office came into view—a corner office. The background was New York City, and skyscrapers that made the IDS Tower look like a farm silo. Secretaries came and went past a fixed camera. Inside the wide office was an old-fashioned wooden desk, like a librarian might have used back in the day, and a thin, white-haired man looking at some papers.

"Trace, can you sit over here?" Carlos asked.

Trace got up and headed toward a chair in front of a fixed cam.

"Also called the hot seat," Tasha said.

Trace mustered a small smile as he settled in, but his armpits went clammy.

"Just be yourself," Laura said. "You'll like Mr. Rupert. Think of him as a grandfather."

Trace looked over to his father, who nodded encouragingly.

"Counting down," Carlos said, tension in his voice. "Five, four, three, two, one—"

A second, closer camera cut to Mr. Rupert at his desk, and a well-dressed younger man, an assistant of some kind, waiting as Mr. Rupert signed some papers. Then the younger guy leaned closer, whispered to Mr. Rupert, and pointed to the camera.

"Oh yeah. It's Minneapolis, yes?" Mr. Rupert said. He blinked as if to focus his eyes.

"That's right, sir," Laura said briskly and cheerfully. "Hello! Laura Williams and Team Blu here."

"Hi there," Mr. Rupert said, leaning back. "I always liked Minneapolis. It's a clean city. People are nice there."

"Thank you, sir," Laura said. "But I miss New York. It's hard to get a good bagel here."

"Everybody wants to work in New York," Mr. Rupert said. "So what are we up to again?"

"Team Blu, sir. Our new energy drink? We're gearing up for the launch."

"I remember now," Mr. Rupert said. "We're going to have a race car and a driver."

"Exactly," Laura said.

"And who talked me into this?" Mr. Rupert said, his eyes narrowing.

Laura laughed nervously. "All of us, sir, including the Chicago office."

"Yes, that's true," Mr. Rupert said. "So what are we up to today?"

"I'd like you to meet our driver," Laura said. "Trace Bonham, meet Mr. Rupert."

Mr. Rupert leaned closer to the camera.

"Hello," Trace said awkwardly.

"Hello to you, young man," Mr. Rupert said.

Trace was silent.

"What kind of race car do you drive?" Mr. Rupert asked.

"A Super Stock, sir."

"This is not NASCAR, right?" Mr. Rupert asked quickly.

"No, sir," Laura interjected. "This is real racing—small town, dirt track. Midwest. That's the centerpiece of our whole ad initiative—"

"Because NASCAR is too rich for my blood," Mr. Rupert continued.

"We all agreed on that, sir," Laura said quickly. "All our research showed—"

"Good," Mr. Rupert said, cutting her off again. "So, son, tell me a little about yourself."

Trace swallowed, and gave him the short version: high school, Headwaters Speedway, driving a grain truck for his summer job.

In the middle of it, Mr. Rupert looked sideways. "Nice-looking, articulate young man," he said to someone out of sight.

Trace paused.

Mr. Rupert turned back to Trace. "So, are you a Ford or a Chevy man?"

"Ford, sir," Trace said.

"I used to have fine old Ford," Mr. Rupert said. "A 1955 Crown Victoria. First year Ford made that model. I worked three jobs to pay for that car—which was pretty fast in its day. Had a big V-8 engine. Ran like a dream."

"1955? Are you sure you didn't have the in-line six-cylinder?" Trace asked.

Beside him, Laura sucked in a short breath.

"Yes—yes it was a six," Mr. Rupert said quickly, a twinkle in his eye. "I remember because I always wished I had waited one more year for that V-8." He waved at Trace and the others. "I think I've seen enough. Best of luck to you, son. Go get 'em, Team Blu!"

"Thank you, sir!" Laura said quickly as the image on the screen shrank to black.

There was silence in the room.

"We did it!" Carlos said.

"Yes!" Laura said, jumping up to high-five Carlos. Then she turned to Trace. "Don't ever scare me like that again!"

"Sorry," Trace said, then realized she was smiling for real.

"Great work, Trace," Tasha said.

"Hey, isn't it lunchtime?" Carlos said.

"I totally agree," Laura said, fanning herself as if overheated and overworked.

Trace did not feel like they had done any work at all.

Lunch was at a café where the waitstaff all wore black and white, and the food was served in very small portions; Trace's plate came with three broiled shrimp and a tiny swirl of red sauce of some kind. He and his father asked more questions: about Trace's responsibilities, about travel, about where they would race, how many shows— and about school.

"School, yes," Laura said. "There will be days during the school year that we'll need you. Tasha will be in touch with your school, your teachers, to make sure everyone's comfortable. We'll arrange for online classes and tutoring."

"Because school has to come first," Don said. He was on his second glass of wine.

"Of course," Laura said. "And we also have to talk about your salary," she said to Trace.

"You mean, I'll really get paid to drive?" he blurted.

The assembled Team Blu laughed loudly.

"Oh dear, we have so much work to do with you," Laura said, reaching over to fluff up Trace's hair, then resting her hand on his shoulder.

Trace's gaze went sideways to her long white fingers and red nail polish.

"Did you notice Mr. Rupert's office? He owns that building," Laura said. "But he owns it because he doesn't buy Learjets or pay outrageous salaries. He's sort of cheap, actually."

Trace nodded.

"Anyway," Laura said, removing her hand to take another sip of her wine, "we'll talk money after lunch."

Which went on for another hour. The adults were very cheerful by then. They didn't return to the offices of Halloran & Peterson until after two p.m. An assistant brought around coffee, as Laura, an attorney named Larry, and Trace and his father sat in a smaller conference room.

Larry went through the liability release forms. "Signature lines are marked by the colored tabs," he said. "Green for Trace, red for Mr. Bonham, yellow for Mrs. Bonham."

"I'll have my attorney look at these, then sign and send them back," Don said.

"Of course," Larry said. "Be aware, also, that your wife's signature will need to be witnessed."

Don looked at him.

"Given the situation," Larry added, with a slight shrug.

"All right," Don said, with a glance to Trace.

"Now on to the fun part," Laura said. She removed some other formal-looking papers and looked down the pages. "This is our contract offer. It's a little complicated, so please take it home and give it a close look. By signing, you agree to drive exclusively for Team Blu."

"Exclusively?" Trace asked.

"No more racing on your own," Larry said.

"You mean—" Trace began, and pulled back from the table.

"We mean that very soon you will have a brand-new Super Stock to drive," Laura said, "complete with a full support team."

"But I can't drive my own race car?"

"That's right," Larry said briskly. "You'll also see a list of other prohibited activities. They include motorcycle riding and/or racing, skateboarding, snowboarding, operation of a personal watercraft such as a WaveRunner or Sea-Doo, and skydiving."

Trace was silent.

"All race car drivers have these restrictions," Laura said. "It's a way for us to protect you and us."

Trace glanced at his dad.

"Since there is a recision period, we'd like to get your signature today," the attorney said. "Once you sign, a whole bunch of administrative things can start to move forward."

"Recision period?" Trace asked.

"It's a window of time, right after you sign something, when you can back out with no penalty," Larry said. "It's standard in the industry."

Trace glanced to his father, who nodded.

"How long do I have—I mean, if I wanted to back out?" Trace asked the attorney.

"Three days."

"I'd like a week," Trace said.

The attorney glanced at Laura, who nodded.

"I think this part will reassure you," she said to Trace. "It's what we're prepared to offer you to be our Team Blu driver." She spun the contract 180 degrees.

Trace's gaze went to the numbers. He laughed.

"What?" Laura said defensively.

Trace's father nudged him hard under the table.

"It looks . . . fine," Trace said. Trying to keep his hand from shaking, he reached for the pen and signed his name in two places.

"Good," Laura said. "Well—we're done for today. A big day for all of us!"

"That's for sure," Trace's dad said, giving Trace a one-armed hug.

Laura waved for Tasha. "Take these contracts, make three copies, each page."

"Sure," Tasha said. Around Laura, she had a fixed smile that didn't much show in her eyes.

"As soon as she brings your copies, we'll get you on your way home," Laura said.

Trace nodded.

"Excuse me—I need to catch Larry for a second," Laura said.

"Sure," Trace answered. He stood quietly with his father; everybody else moved on.

"Can you believe it?" his father whispered. "That's college money. For driving a race car!"

Trace was silent. He could smell red wine on his father's breath. He turned to look out the tall windows. People on the street below looked like fleas. An ambulance worked its way through traffic, red light flashing, siren fainter than a mosquito's whine. Traffic was thick and unyielding; the ambulance swung left, then right, like a race car trying to find its way among slower cars.

"Here we go," Tasha said. She came up alongside the glass and held out the contracts.

"Thanks." As Trace reached for them, he flinched. Just outside the glass was a flash—an explosion, a puff of smoke. Not smoke, but feathers.

Tasha shook her head. "Another pigeon bites the dust."

Gray and blue feathers floated, then swirled sideways in wind currents around the building. The falcon reappeared from below, flapping upward, carrying a limp pigeon toward the nest.

"Like I said, you don't want to watch," Tasha said. "And anyway, your car is ready down below."

6

On Saturday, Trace showed up at Headwaters Speedway without his Street Stock and trailer. As he drove along pit row, heads turned. Drivers and crew members looked his way. Some smiled and threw Trace a thumbs-up sign; others just stared, then turned away.

Trace parked his Ford truck in his usual slot next to the Harkness family—who had already fudged halfway over into Trace's space.

"Hey, hey, hey, Mr. Big Shot!" Gerry called.

"Hey, boss."

"Heard you got that ride!" Gerry said. He stuck out a big paw that rocked Trace as they shook hands.

"Yeah. But now I've got nothing to do for a couple of weeks until my car's ready," Trace said.

"You can crew for me," Gerry said.

"We probably can't afford him now," Gerry's wife called; she looked up from her tire grooving.

"They actually gonna pay you?" Gerry asked, leaning closer.

"Looks that way."

"Decent?" Gerry added, lowering his voice.

"It'll beat running a grain truck," Trace answered, and moved over to look at Gerry's old Super Stock.

"Worked all week on this beast," Gerry said proudly. He put both hands on the fender. "Fresh heads, rebuilt carb. We're ready to bend some metal tonight."

"So let's hear how it sounds," Trace said.

Gerry's wife slipped into the car and fired the engine. Trace leaned close over the motor and worked the throttle linkage. The 360-cubic-inch Chevy growled like an unhappy dog on a choke chain. Trace turned one ear, then the other toward the engine. It was hard to explain, but he heard slightly different things in each ear.

"You like?" Gerry shouted.

Trace was silent. He let the throttle spring pull the rpm back to idle speed. "There's a teeny little dead spot."

Gerry lit a cigarette.

"You rebuilt the carb yourself?" Trace asked.

Gerry nodded.

"Let's take a look at it," Trace said, motioning for Cindy to kill the engine. After lifting off the round air cleaner, Trace shone a flashlight into the carburetor. Gerry paced behind, smoking.

"Speedway Motors had a special on new carbs," Gerry's wife said. "Could have had it here overnight, but Mr. Mechanic had to do it himself."

"I saved two hundred bucks!" Gerry exclaimed. "Most wives would be happy about that."

"Most wives are not your crew chief. You win a race, your check pays for a new carb."

"Did you replace the gaskets?" Trace asked.

Gerry looked away, across the pits, and took a long draw on his cigarette.

"That would be a negatory," his wife said.

"I ask because I'm seeing some tiny flakes showing up," Trace said. "Those gaskets disintegrate after a while. Got any carb cleaner?"

Gerry dispatched Tim to the parts trailer. Soon Trace aimed a spray can's plastic nozzle into the open carb, and drowned it with spray—then signaled to Cindy to fire the engine. After a couple of cycles of spraying and choking, the carburetor gradually turned shiny inside—and the throttle lag disappeared.

"That should do it," Trace said, wiping his hands as he stepped back from the Super Stock. "You'll need to replace your fuel filter real soon—it's going to pick up those gasket flakes—but filters are cheap."

"Like him," Cindy said, with a glance to Gerry.

"One hundred bucks on my labor, though," Trace said, holding out his hand.

"Put it on my bill, Mr. Big Shot," Gerry said.

Trace walked down pit row. Beau Kim had found a real

beater of a Mod-Four, and was adjusting the front-end suspension. "Hey, Trace," Beau said, "how does my toe-in look?"

Trace stepped to the front of Beau's car, then backed off several paces, and knelt down to look. "Your front tires are still going in different directions. Keep cranking 'em in."

Beau leaned back to fit his wrench to the nut on the suspension arm.

Trace walked on, passing Amber Jenkins's Mod-Four. With her crew of brothers, she didn't need any help, but she spotted him and waved him over.

"Congrats, dude!" she said, throwing him a short, hard hug. "You're gonna make us all proud."

"Thanks," Trace said. "No pressure, right?"

Amber laughed, then her eyes turned serious. "Could you listen to my little pony? There's something funny going on."

"I'm not really a four-cylinder guy," Trace said, but she was already reaching in to fire the engine.

Trace listened. The 2.3-liter Ford whined like a tomcat. A four-cylinder motor had a higher-pitched call than a V-8, but this little cat had a porcupine quill stuck in its throat. Trace immediately signaled Amber to kill the engine.

"What?" she asked quickly.

"You've got some kind of valve problem," Trace said. "Not big, but it will be."

Amber's brothers looked at one another. "What did I tell you?" one of them said.

"So why didn't you pop the head off and look?" the other shot back. "You had all damn day!"

"Hey, hey, hey!" Amber said.

"Do you use drop-in valve springs?" Trace asked.

"Yes," the brothers all said at once.

"You might have a broken spring, and maybe just a keeper missing. But I wouldn't send her out there as is."

"Get that head off, right now!" barked Joe, the oldest brother and the crew chief. The brothers converged on Amber's engine like ER doctors around a bleeding patient.

"Thanks," Amber said to Trace.

"Hey, it's what I do," he answered.

"No, you drive a Super Stock now," Amber said, giving him a one-handed high five, "and don't you forget it."

Trace walked around to the grandstand to watch the heats. It felt odd being on this side of the racetrack. No crew to hang out with, just himself wandering around. He walked over to Ritchie's BBQ Waggin. In line in front of him, a large woman wearing a bright Danny Lasoski sprint car T-shirt peered closely at a sheet of paper. It was the current Headwaters Speedway points standings; on the sheet she had made small, careful notes in pencil. Then she compared today's sheet with last week's. She had a notebook full of them—the entire season's standings, week by week.

She sensed Trace's gaze, and turned to look; she had very thick glasses that needed cleaning.

"If Gerry places third or better in the rest of the Super Stock features, he'll beat that Bialachek for fifth place," she said. She said "Gerry" as if she was a close friend.

"It could happen," Trace offered.

"I don't like that No. 28," the woman said. "Something about him just rubs me the wrong way, you know what I mean? Same with Steve Kinser and Dale Jr.—I've never liked those guys."

Trace couldn't think of a good reply, but the lady began to make more tiny notes on her sheet and the line moved forward.

Ritchie and Winona couldn't have been happier for Trace. "You're gonna miss my barbecue!" Ritchie said, his cheeks scarlet from the heat.

"No doubt," Trace said. At the till, Ritchie's step-daughter, Tudy, rolled her eyes. Before Trace handed over his money, she quickly wiped her face and tucked a strand of hair behind her ear.

"Thanks," he said.

She gave him a shy smile.

He wanted to say something to her, like "You're not gonna be selling barbecue all your life." He had always thought that about Tudy; certain people had a style about them that said "This part of my life is just temporary. I've got way better stuff to come." But Leonard the basketball player was sitting in the back of the trailer, so Trace didn't say anything more to Tudy. He and Leonard exchanged nods.

Carrying his barbecue basket, Trace moved through the crowd toward the stands. Patrick came past carrying a stack of toilet paper rolls; he was headed to the men's john.

"Hey, Trace!" Patrick called. He was unembarrassed about stopping in a crowd, his arms full of toilet paper.

"Working?" Trace asked. Dumb question.

"The usual," Patrick said with a shrug.

They were silent for a moment.

"You want to drive my Street Stock?" Trace asked. The question—the whole idea—came out of nowhere.

"Say again?" Patrick asked.

Trace paused to make sure he wasn't totally crazy. He felt strange today, a little out of body, but this idea was not crazy. And maybe it wasn't out of nowhere. It had something to do with what people like Patrick and Tudy had in life versus what they deserved a chance at. "I said, would you like to drive my Street Stock?"

Patrick stared. He cocked his head. "Drive it where?"

"On the racetrack, numbnuts."

"Are you kidding?" Patrick asked.

"No. It's just sitting there. Somebody should drive it."

The rolls of toilet paper dropped from Patrick's hands and bounced away like escaping cottontails. "Me, race your Street Stock?" he asked, his eyes widening. A huge grin broke across his face.

"Why not?" Trace said.

"Well, I mean, what about Tyler? Or your friends from school?"

"Those guys could put together a race car if they really wanted to," Trace said. "They're motor heads. You aren't."

Patrick was silent. "You're serious, aren't you?" he suddenly asked.

"Yes. What's to stop you?" Trace asked.

As quickly as he had smiled, Patrick frowned. "My parents, to start."

"Hey, can we get some toilet paper in here?" a man shouted from the doorway to the men's room.

Trace knelt, picked up a roll, and pitched a strike to the guy—who caught it and disappeared inside. Patrick didn't turn.

"We can deal with your parents," Trace said.

"I don't think so," Patrick said, scratching his head again. "My mother would come unglued."

Trace was silent. Then he said, "Do they ever come to the track?"

"No," Patrick said.

"So how would they find out?" Trace asked. "There are only three regular shows left in the season—and it's not like you're going to win. By the time they hear that you're racing—if they ever do—you'll be done for the year."

"I'll be done for more than a year if they find out," Patrick murmured.

"What are the chances that they'll find out?" Trace said. "Look around. Do you see any of your parents' friends here?"

"Are you kidding?" Patrick asked as his eyes scanned the crowd.

"There you go," Trace said.

"What about your dad?" Patrick said suddenly. "Would it be all right with him?"

"I'll deal with him—don't worry about that," Trace said.

"Whoa," Patrick said, his smile returning. "Me in a race car!"

Carrying his food, Trace headed on up the wood stairs to the grandstand. The worn planks were filled with die-hard fans in padded stadium seats; kids squirming in their parents' arms; punksters with piercings and Mohawk haircuts; young and tanned mothers swelling out of tank tops; tradesmen with sun-creased faces and battered fingernails; bikers wearing bandannas; a few grizzled Vietnam vets; and lots of white-haired, suntanned older couples who came every Saturday night and ate their supper— Ritchie's barbecue—at the track.

Trace made sure not to look up toward the announcer's booth, but sat where Mel might see him. Two rows down and to the side, a youngish guy with a couple of little screamers and a large wife, either pregnant or fat, talked loudly about the local cars.

"Mod-Fours are too lightweight for me," the loud guy said. "Give me a Modified or a Super Stock any day." Another, better-dressed young couple sat next to him.

"Do you race?" the woman asked politely. Trace guessed that the two guys had gone to high school together; the first (the loud guy) had stayed around town, the other had moved away. Now both guys were married.

"Used to," the local guy said, with a glance to his wife.

"I'm gonna get back in it one of these days. I'm gonna get me a car again."

"Brent races lawn mowers now," the large wife said.

"Excuse me?" the other wife asked. She laughed, then covered her mouth.

"That's right," Brent said. "Lawn mowers. It's getting to be a big deal. Haven't you seen it on the Speed Channel? There's different classes—stock lawn mowers, modified lawn mowers—just like here." He gestured to the cars on the track.

"That's . . . really something," the woman said. She was fit and trim, and had nice brown legs in a short khaki skirt.

"You should come watch him race sometime," the heavyset wife said. "Our kids love it."

"Brent had a 1972 Camaro back in the day," the other guy said.

"Back in the day," Brent repeated. He looked at the cars on the track, and beyond, to the pits, the drivers, and their crews.

When the heats ended, throngs of people headed down the stairs for food and a bathroom break. Someone had left a newspaper; so as not to look stupid sitting alone, Trace picked it up. Glanced through it. There was an article on the Perseid meteor shower, which was peaking right now. Suddenly he felt Mel behind him, or, rather, smelled her—her signature scent: vanilla or peach mixed with coconut sunscreen.

"So what's it feel like to be over here?" she said, settling down next to him.

He smiled behind his sunglasses. "Strange."

They looked across the track in silence.

"I'm sorry I was bitchy to those people from Team Blu," Mel said.

"Don't worry about it," Trace said.

"I guess I was a little mad at them," she said.

"Mad? Why would you be mad?" Trace asked, turning to her.

Mel wouldn't look at him. "Because you won't be racing here anymore."

Trace swallowed. "Headwaters will always be my home track," he began.

"No it won't," she said, looking down to the worn boards beneath her feet. "Something just ended."

"Nothing just ended," Trace said. He covered her nearest hand with his.

"Are you sure?" she asked. She didn't pull her fingers away.

He could only nod at her.

"Well, that's settled then," she said, with a quick smile, and pulled away.

"You want to get a Dairy Queen after the races?" Trace asked. With Mel it was important not to think too long about things—just say them.

"Maybe. Sure, why not?" she said.

"Great," Trace said, then dried up on words completely.

"Okay. Well, I should get back to the booth," she said, standing up.

"Okay," Trace said again, dumbly. Why was it that his vocabulary shrank to zero when she was near?

"Hey, I saw you talking with Patrick," Mel said.

"Oh yeah," Trace said. "Just . . . guy stuff."

"Yeah, right," Mel said.

"We were discussing toilet paper," Trace said. "Big rolls or little sheets—what's best."

"What's best is what's cheapest," Mel threw back.

Trace watched her tanned legs scissor her up the bleachers to the announcer's booth, where she disappeared inside. Its wide window was tinted. As Trace turned back to the track, he felt her eyes on his shoulders. Or maybe it was the late, soft orange sunlight.

Gerry Harkness won the Super Stock feature—his first win of the season—but Trace couldn't say who won the other classes. He was thinking about Dairy Queens.

After the races, he waited outside the grandstand. Haulers large and small left with their race cars on trailers or buttoned up inside. Fans lingered and talked to the local drivers. The large lady Trace had encountered in line at Ritchie's Waggin stood out of the light a few paces from Gerry Harkness; a group of well-wishers had gathered around him, and big Gerry was laughing and shaking hands. The woman fussed with her program, but leaned in slightly, eavesdropping.

Trace walked over to Gerry and stuck out his hand. "Now who's famous?"

"Hey, kid, did you see those last two laps?" Gerry boomed.

"Yeah, great," Trace said, hoping Gerry wouldn't quiz him.

"That baby ran like a dream tonight," Gerry said, throwing a quick headlock on Trace.

"Just sign over that first-place check to me," Trace said.

"As if you'll need it!" Gerry said.

"Hey, there's somebody I want you to meet," Trace said, nodding toward the shadows. To the side, the big lady's eyes widened as Trace came toward her with Gerry. She looked ready to bolt.

"Hi again," Trace said to her. "We talked in line. At Ritchie's Waggin?"

"We did?" she asked.

"I didn't get your name, though," Trace said.

"It's Margaret. Margie," she stammered.

"Margie, I'd like you to meet Gerry Harkness."

"Hi there, Margie," Gerry said easily, and stuck out a big hand.

"Wow!" the woman said. She giggled. "I don't know what to say!"

"She's a big fan of yours," Trace said.

"You've got to beat that No. 28 guy, Bialachek!" Margie blurted.

Gerry smiled big. "I'll try my darndest," he said.

There was a moment of silence.

"Could you sign this?" Margie asked, holding out her points standing sheet. "I mean, if it ain't any bother."

"No problem," Gerry said, patting his shirt for a pen.

"Use mine," Margie said quickly.

Gerry carefully wrote his name on her program.

"Thanks!" Margie said, and hurried away.

Off to the side, Cindy Harkness shook her head. "Now who's famous?" she repeated. Gerry laughed.

Just then the track's infield lights went out. People turned to their cars, and the Harkness family headed to their school-bus hauler. Soon it was just Trace, waiting alone near the ticket booth.

Finally Mel appeared. "I had this weird idea you might not wait," she said.

"Why wouldn't I?"

"I thought maybe I scared you off."

"You did a little—but in a good way," Trace added quickly.

"Let's go before I change my mind," she said. She glanced around the grounds as if she was forgetting something.

"My truck's over here," Trace said.

In town, they sat in Trace's Ford and ate their Blizzards and watched the people. The Dairy Queen was always busy after the races.

"What about your mom?" Mel asked.

"What about her?" Trace replied. Mothers—mothers who were gone—something they had in common.

"I mean, what does she think of this Team Blu thing?"

Trace was silent. "We haven't told her yet."

"Oh dear," Mel said.

Trace shrugged.

"Men," Mel said. "So when *are* you going to tell her?"

"Soon. We have to go down to Eau Claire and have her sign the release papers so I can drive."

"What if she won't sign?"

"She'll sign," Trace said, glancing down the highway.

Mel stopped eating. "I wouldn't," she said.

"Huh?" Trace asked.

"If you were my son, and I saw those Team Blu people—especially that creepy Laura—I would never sign."

Trace laughed. "She's not that creepy."

"That lipstick, those red fingernails? She was scary."

"You're a little scary sometimes," Trace said.

"I am?" Mel asked. Her eyes widened with surprise.

Trace nodded.

"How?"

He shrugged. "It's like you're always getting several channels at once. I never quite know what to say to you."

"Which is why you don't talk much?"

He was silent.

"It's true," she said suddenly, and let her shoulders slump. "I need to be nicer and not so prickly and demanding and sarcastic at times. I don't listen well. I don't let people finish their sentences. I'm not a very nice person."

"No, you just have a lot of responsibility. Very few high school girls run a speedway."

Mel shrugged.

"Your dad would be lost without you," Trace said.

Mel turned to him. "What about you?"

Trace swallowed. "Me too."

Their eyes met. She shivered. "I always get cold after eating ice cream," she said, and moved over next to him.

Soon their spoons clattered on the bottom of their containers. Trace made sure not to suck loudly on his straw.

"Now what?" Mel said.

"Well," Trace said, "there's always the meteor shower."

"Huh?" Mel asked.

"The Perseid meteor shower. It happens every year at this time in August when the earth passes through the tail of the Swift-Tuttle comet. But we'll need to go somewhere where it's really dark."

Mel raised an eyebrow. "Are you some kind of astronomer?"

Trace grinned. "No. I swear I'm telling the truth."

"Okay. We can go somewhere for a little while, but we'd better see some meteors," Mel said.

"Guaranteed," Trace said, crossing his fingers as he started the engine.

They drove east of town, leaving the glow of city lights behind, to an old gravel pit. Tall cones of sand rose up like the outlines of pyramids. Because the sand and gravel were all around, and there were no ponds or water, there would be fewer mosquitoes.

"Is this where you bring all your girlfriends?" Mel asked.

"No," Trace said. "I come here once in a while to target-shoot."

"By yourself?"

"Usually."

"You do a lot of things by yourself," Mel said.

Trace had no answer for that.

"Okay. So which way are we supposed to look for these meteors?" Mel said.

"North," Trace said, and parked accordingly.

They got out of the truck and climbed on the hood, then leaned back against the windshield.

"I'm waiting," Mel said. The night light of moon and stars glinted on her teeth.

Trace edged closer.

"For falling stars," she said.

Trace stopped just close enough so that their shoulders and legs touched. They watched the vast, light-pricked blackness.

"Not seeing meteors," Mel said.

"So let's do the constellations," Trace said. He actually knew some from an old kids' book. "There's Ursa Major, the Bear."

"Where?"

Trace leaned in almost cheek to cheek with her, took

her finger, and pointed it skyward. "There. It has a long, narrow body, legs, and then a tail that goes up behind. See it?"

"No. I can never see them!" Mel said. "I just don't get constellations. It's some kind of failure of my imagination."

"No, it's more like connecting the dots, but you do have to imagine the lines between the stars," Trace said. "You see the nose, right?"

"No," Mel murmured.

He leaned closer. Her breath was sweet from the ice cream, and warm. She kept looking upward; Trace looked only at her—at the side of her face, the smoothness of her cheek. Her ear, with the swirl of hair around it, looked like the Milky Way.

Clumsily, he put his arm around her.

"What are you doing?" she asked suddenly—and pulled away.

"Sorry," Trace said quickly.

She was silent. She put a closed hand to her mouth and looked down.

"I didn't mean to—" he began.

"No, it's not you, it's me," she said. Her shoulders twitched. She was beginning to cry.

"Hey, don't do that," Trace said. He reached out his hand to her face. This time she didn't flinch.

"You're leaving, that's why we can't—why it has to be 'just friends.' "

"Why 'just friends'?" Trace blurted.

"Because you're leaving!" she said, anger in her voice. "No girl with half a brain would want to get involved with you right now—just before you go on the road. I know what the life of a race car driver is like. I've heard the stories from my dad. Look at any NASCAR or Nextel race on television, not at the cars, but at the women hanging around. Women love drivers. They're like wolves. That's going to be your life!"

"Team Blu is not NASCAR or Nextel," Trace said. "It's midwest dirt track."

"Same difference," she said, sliding off the hood and onto the ground. "Put a guy in a racing suit, especially someone as handsome as you"—she looked down—"and the girls will be there."

"I'm not going to be that kind of driver."

She looked at him for a long moment—a moment when everything or nothing could happen. "We should go," she said.

After he dropped her off, Trace drove slowly home. A half mile ahead on the gravel road was the farm, its mercury-vapor yard light glinting off the grain bins, but he wasn't ready to be home yet.

He stopped the truck where the fields were dark, turned off the engine, and let the radio play, a classic country station. He leaned back in the seat and watched the black sky. Within seconds, a meteor streaked low and fiery, like a giant tracer bullet, across the northern sky.

Not a minute later an even bigger one lanced yellow and orange along the same path—so brightly that he imagined he heard its sizzle and fizz as it cut through the atmosphere. Maybe that was the way to drive: fast, hard, and alone, like a falling star.

 **7**

"Don't you think you might have told me about this sooner?" his mother asked.

"Maybe," Trace answered. He had finally called her. He shifted his phone to the other ear.

"I mean, how long have you known?" she pressed.

"A few days," Trace said.

"But you said the tryouts were two weeks ago."

"I didn't know I'd be chosen. So I thought, Why say anything until I know for sure?" Trace replied.

His mother was silent. If there was anything that worked for her, it was logic.

"I didn't want to make a big deal about it until I had all the facts," he continued. *All the facts* was a phrase stolen straight from his mom. Whenever Trace had gotten in trouble as a kid, his mother—not his dad—first wanted to hear "all the facts," then decide upon the appropriate punishment.

"But now it does sound like a big deal," she said, her voice softening just a bit.

"It might be, yes," Trace said. It was funny how he could feel both of his parents inside his head at the same time. His father was the excitable one, the risk taker in business, the mover and shaker; his mother was the supremely logical one. She made the original *Star Trek* guy Dr. Spock, with the pointy ears, look wild and crazy. But no doubt about it, Trace's personality tilted more toward his mother.

It was a miracle that she and his father had ever gotten married. There must have been a moment (the logical part of his brain at work here) when both of them were ready, when it was time to be married. It really didn't matter to whom—the nearest attractive person was fine.

"What about school?" she asked.

"Covered. It came up right away during the meeting. They will be talking to my teachers and will arrange for online classes and tutoring."

"Meeting? What meeting?"

Trace sucked in a breath. Big mistake. He went ahead and told her.

"I could have driven over to Minneapolis," she said.

"You could have stayed home with Dad and me—and then you'd actually know what was going on," Trace replied.

There was silence on the other end. It was several seconds before she spoke again.

"I think you and your dad should drive down here and we can talk about this—as a family." Her voice sounded smaller. Wounded. Like he had hurt her badly.

Trace bit his lip. "I agree," he said.

At Sam's, a steak house in town, his father finished some calls on his cell phone, then turned to Trace. "We'll leave tomorrow," he said. They were having their supper out (they usually ate out). "First thing in the morning. We've got to get those release forms signed."

Trace was silent. He couldn't disagree. After all, the recision period was over; Trace was now Team Blu's driver—unless of course his mother wouldn't sign. Tasha and now Laura were calling every day about the release forms.

"She'll sign," his father said, reading his mind. "Once she sees the numbers, once she sees what they're going to pay you, we'll have her."

Trace glanced at his father, then back to his food.

"You know what I mean," his father added quickly.

Trace picked at his food. The burger was dry, the fries floppy. He remembered his favorite hot dish, "cheesy macs," which his mother used to make all the time when he was small. For one instant, a thought struck him: maybe she wouldn't sign. Maybe she'd come home and take back her old job, and she and his father could find their way back together, and they would be a normal family again. Whatever that was.

"Check," his father called to the waiter.

On the way down to Eau Claire, a six-hour drive, they were passing through Amery, Wisconsin, when Tasha called. "The car's done," she said, excitement in her voice. "They're finishing up the lettering today."

"What number?"

"It will be No. 18x," she replied. "Do you like it?"

Trace was silent.

"You still there?" Tasha asked.

"It's a racing thing. No driver wants a number that reads right upside down."

Tasha laughed. Then she said, "Seriously?"

"Yes," Trace said.

"Man, I've got a lot to learn about this racing business."

"So where's the car right now?" Trace asked.

"At a specialty lettering shop just outside of Minneapolis," Tasha said. "But I know we can't change the number at this point."

"I can live with it," Trace said. "I'm not totally superstitious."

"Sorry," Tasha said. "We should have consulted you."

"So what was the holdup on the car, anyway?" Trace asked, happy to change the subject.

"It was all the engine builder. Some older guy, a motor wizard of some kind, who only works when he's 'feeling it.' "

"I like him already," Trace said.

"Bernard 'Smoky' Lyle," Tasha said. "Know him?"

"No," Trace said. "I'll try looking him up online."

"I Googled him, but no luck," Tasha said.

"How'd you come up with him and the Peabody chassis shop in the first place?" Trace asked. He could talk to Tasha all day.

"Beats me. I'm just a worker bee," Tasha said. "Speaking of which, we're still waiting for those release forms with your mother's signature. You're making us a little nervous here, kid."

"I'll be seeing her tonight," Trace answered. "You worry too much."

"That's what they pay me for," Tasha said. "Worrying."

In Eau Claire, Trace and his father checked in to a Super 8 motel. It was a nonsmoking room, heavily scented with carpet powder to mask the fact that it had once been a smoking room. They showered; then his father had a short nap while Trace watched the Speed Channel. And soon it was time to meet with his mother.

Mike's Smokehouse on Clairemont Avenue was a Texas rib joint, a nice gesture on his mother's part: she didn't eat meat. Trace and his father got there six minutes early and waited in the foyer. Trace checked his cell phone clock against the restaurant's clock. As its minute hand touched the top of the hour—six o'clock—Trace took in a breath and held it. He turned to face the door, which pushed open even as he watched.

"Trace, honey!" she said, and hurried forward to hug him.

She felt thinner and harder, but was wearing a perfume that softened her hard edges. She had shorter hair, lightly colored. He let her cling to him, and patted her back. It had been over a month since he had seen her.

Then she let him go and turned to Trace's dad. "Hello, Don," she said. Her eyes were the same flat blue, as if she was weighing the facts, adding things up.

"Hello, Sharon," he said.

They made no move to hug or shake hands. The silence went on.

"Shall we?" Trace said, gesturing toward the tables.

Trace's mother ordered only a salad, light on oil and vinegar dressing. Trace ordered light, too; he was never very hungry at the table with both parents. His father ordered the biggest steak on the menu. The first half hour was mainly small talk: Trace's friends, life "up north." Then, gradually, the conversation turned to racing. Trace filled her in on the tryouts, the meeting in Minneapolis, the whole Team Blu thing.

"But why you?" she pressed, looking at Trace. "Forgive me, dear, but it's not like you're a famous driver."

"That's just it," Trace's father said impatiently, stabbing his fork into a hunk of porterhouse steak (rare). "Their goal is take an unknown talent, somebody without baggage, and use that to promote a new product."

"Use *him* to promote a new product," Trace's mother corrected.

"All right, *him*," Trace's father said, with a glance at Trace.

"And how do you feel about this?" she asked, turning to Trace.

He shrugged. "Okay." He didn't want to get caught in the middle of anything.

"It's a dream opportunity," Trace's father said, chewing loudly. "No two ways about that."

"I want to hear it from Trace," his mother said, ignoring his father.

Trace paused, then said, "It's sort of like that. Sometimes when I wake up in the morning, I'm pretty sure I dreamt it."

They were all silent.

"And you'll get paid for this?"

"Yes."

Trace's dad reached down, unsnapped his briefcase, and brought out the contract and the release forms. He pushed the contract across the table to Trace's mom.

Her eyes skimmed the pages, then went to the bottom of the last page. "Are you kidding?" she asked, leaning back from the table. She laughed.

"This is not a joke. This is big time," Don said. "It's not NASCAR, but it's a lot of money to race a Super Stock on dirt."

She stared at them. First one, then the other. "I feel really stupid," she said.

Trace glanced at his dad, then back to his mom.

"Why?" Trace asked.

"To be honest, I've never understood the whole racing thing," she said. "It's expensive, it's loud, it's dirty. The people I've seen in the pits are always dusty and rough. They smoke, they have bad teeth, they love that horrible racetrack food. The whole sport is sort of ridiculous—cars chasing each other around and around in a circle, and they never really go anywhere." She paused. "I feel stupid, because clearly I must be missing something."

Trace's father shrugged. "That's like long-distance running, for me. I don't get why anybody would run marathons. I mean, I understand the exercise part, but when is enough enough? You pound along all by yourself for twenty-six miles. At least in the car world we talk to people."

"Anyway," Trace said quickly to his mother, "I need you to sign the release forms. In front of a witness."

His mother stared at the papers. For one of the few times in his memory, she seemed lost. Upended. Indecisive.

"Will you be safe?" she said.

"He'll have only the best equipment," his father said. "He'll be way safer than driving his old Street Stock."

"And school?" she asked.

"Covered," Trace said. "I'll graduate with my class, just like normal. I'll take the SATs on schedule. I'll go to college somewhere, I promise."

"How much will you be traveling?" she asked.

"Quite a lot," Trace said.

"What about your friends back home?"

"They're excited for me. Like I hoped you would be," Trace said.

She stared at him for a long moment—then swallowed. She shifted her gaze to the papers. "All right, I'll do it," she said. Then she began to cry.

8

Back at the motel after dinner, Trace and his dad faxed the release forms to the Team Blu office in Minneapolis. The motel clerk, a young woman with black hair and lots of tiny holes up the sides of her ears, was uncertain about operating the fax machine. Trace's dad talked her through it. Afterward, in their stinky-clean room, he said to Trace, "Better call your friend Tasha to make sure those forms got there."

" 'My friend Tasha'? What's that supposed to mean?"

"Nothing," Trace's dad said. "I mean, you two seem to get along well. That's all."

Trace gave him a look.

"Hey, she's a great girl," his father said.

"You noticed," Trace said. He flipped open his phone.
Tasha answered on the first ring.

"Don't you ever go home?" Trace asked.

"This is advertising," Tasha said. "We never sleep. And yes, your forms came through. I gave them to Laura. She'll be in touch about hooking up with the car. You're still in Eau Claire, right?"

"Yes."

"Hang on a sec—" Tasha said. Trace could hear Laura's voice, quick and sharp, in the background.

He listened but couldn't pick up much.

"She wants you at the Princeton, Minnesota, speedway tomorrow afternoon to meet the crew and see the car," Tasha said.

"Okay," Trace said; his grasshoppers tickled their wings inside his stomach.

"One p.m. You need directions?"

"Been there," Trace said. "It's just east of St. Cloud on Highway 169."

"Well, all right. Sleep tight, then," Tasha said, that smile in her voice again.

"Yeah, sure," Trace replied.

Thanks to his father's snoring plus people slamming doors in the hallway, Trace could not sleep. He watched the Speed Channel with the sound turned off. Sprint cars surged around and around the track in Knoxville, Iowa.

Without the noise of engines, the roof-winged cars did look a little strange—like miniatures zipping around a slot car track. At some level, his mother was right: race cars just went around and around in circles.

In the morning he awoke to the biting hum of his father's electric razor. "Up and at 'em, Son," his dad said cheerfully.

Trace groaned.

"Big day ahead."

"Yeah, yeah," Trace said. "Just tell me when you're done in there so I can shower."

"It's all yours," Don said. His son didn't move. "Hey, Trace!"

Trace sat upright in bed. "Whoa!"

His father stared. "Did you think you were dreaming again?"

Trace hurried to the shower, where the hot water burned away the last of his sleep. He leaned out of the curtain and the steaming fog. "How far is Princeton?" he called.

"We've got plenty of time," his dad called back. Trace saw him in the mirror; he was on the phone.

"Say hi to Linda," he said.

"Just take your shower," his dad threw back.

They drove a short two hours to Minneapolis, then another hour north to Princeton. They arrived early. His father pulled into an Arby's.

"I'm not all that hungry," Trace said. He made no move to get out of the pickup.

His father nodded. "Nervous?"

"Noooooo," Trace said sarcastically.

His dad smiled a little. "Once or twice in your life you get to be the tail that wags the dog. This is your time. It doesn't last forever, so try to enjoy it."

"What if I wreck?" Trace blurted. "Like in my first race?"

"You wreck, you wreck. You got a crew behind you. If they're any good, they should have the car back as good as new the next day."

"Speaking of cars, would you mind if one of my friends drove the Street Stock?" Trace asked.

"Up home you mean?" his father replied.

Trace nodded. "Finish out the season at Headwaters."

His father was silent a moment. "Which friend?"

"Patrick Fletcher."

Don stared. "The kid who sings the national anthem?"

"Him," Trace said.

His father laughed. "Are you serious?"

"Yes. It would be fun for everybody. Plus, he's not going to drive fast enough to wreck or hurt himself."

Trace's father blinked rapidly, which meant he was thinking. "He'd have to get registered with WISSOTA. Get a driver's number."

"No big deal. I'll help him with that," Trace said.

His father's brown eyes brightened, and he grinned. "I like it," he said. "Why not? Life should be fun."

———

At a tasteful ten minutes before one p.m., Trace and his father pulled into the Princeton Speedway. Who was at the open gate with her clipboard but Tasha.

"Right on time, thank you!" she said. She gave them each a quick, strong handshake and a smile.

"This is Minnesota," Trace's dad said. "Minnesotans are always on time."

"Maybe that explains why we're two weeks behind on our car," Tasha said, glancing behind at the empty parking lot.

"No comment," Trace's dad said.

"The idea here today is that Trace meets the crew, and tries out the car," Tasha said.

Trace's eyes widened. "I don't have my stuff," he said quickly. "My suit, my helmet, gloves, shoes . . ."

"Got you covered," Tasha said. "Why do you think they pay me the big bucks?"

At that moment the sound of a big truck, downshifting, turned their heads.

"On time. Amazing," Tasha murmured.

The shiny Freightliner tractor—the new model with aerodynamic lines—rumbled slowly into the parking lot, chrome stacks and grillwork flashing in the sunlight. A Coronado model long-haul with a big sleeper cab, the whole thing was painted blue to match the giant trailer. As the rig turned, the tall "stacker" trailer kept coming and coming—as if sliding out of the sky.

"Holy smokes," Trace's dad said.

"Thank you, Mr. Rupert," Tasha said softly.

Behind the tractor-trailer came a smaller, old-school Gulf Stream motor home with darkly tinted windows all around. "That would be your engine guy, Mr. Smoky," Tasha said.

The huge rig eased past them at crawl speed, as if the driver hated to get the chrome wheels dusty. Air brakes hissed, then chirped as they locked; the diesel engine fell off to idle speed and stayed there at a low clatter.

The rider's side thudded. A skinny, younger guy in sunglasses, black T-shirt, blue jeans, and a cell phone on his belt came around the front of the tractor. He stomped the earth, as if testing its firmness, with a scuffed cowboy boot. "Yankee dirt. Never thought it would happen to me," he said with a strong Southern accent.

"You must be Jimmy," Tasha said, stepping forward to shake hands.

"Jimmy Joe Peabody, at your service. You gotta be Tasha."

"That's me," she said.

Jimmy grinned without taking off his glasses. He had good teeth that weren't going to be good forever unless he started brushing. "Thought we was in Canada!" he said.

The driver's door swung open, and an older, thicker version of Jimmy climbed down. With a red do-rag, gray ponytail, and faded black Lynyrd Skynyrd T-shirt, he looked like an old biker—or a roadie for the band.

"Canada? Yeah, right. My boy don't know his directions. He don't even know the states," the man said to Trace's group. "That's what public education gets you these days."

"You must be Harlan Peabody?" Tasha asked.

"That's right, girl," Harlan said, stepping forward to shake hands.

Tasha paused a moment, then shook his hand.

"Well, here we all are. I'd like you *boys* to meet your driver," Tasha said.

Trace stepped forward. "Hey," he said to Jimmy.

Jimmy lifted his sunglasses, leaned left and then right, as if to see better. "They said you was a pretty boy, but I'm not seeing it." He stuck out a hand. "Just kidding, Trace."

"Don't listen to Jimmy—ever," Harlan said, rocking his son out of the way with a big forearm.

"Howdy," Trace said, and tried to match Harlan's crushing grip. He turned. "This is my dad, Don Bonham."

"Hey, Pops," Harlan said good-naturedly. "Really, you do got a handsome boy here."

"He's a pretty good driver, too," Don said without smiling.

"We'll see about that," Harlan drawled.

A slight clacking sound drew their eyes to the motor home; a sliding window, narrowly opened, went shut.

"Smoky, our motor man," Harlan said.

"Can we meet him?" Tasha asked. "We've heard a lot about him. Trace has some questions, I know."

Harlan's ruddy face fell into a pained look. "I don't

think so. Not right now, anyway. Smoky's not a daylight kinda guy."

The motor home with the black windows remained silent and still.

"So what's the skinny, what's the haps here today?" Jimmy asked Tasha. He was a jumpy, twitchy guy.

Tasha glanced at her clipboard. "You show Trace around—the trailer, his quarters, the equipment, the whole traveling thing. Then he tries out the car."

"Now you're talking, girl," Harlan said. "Jimmy—"

"Yes, boss?" Jimmy replied.

"The circus is in town. Let loose the animals!"

Jimmy disappeared around the far side, and soon could be heard thumping around inside the trailer.

"He's not that slow," Harlan said. "The boy does know a thing or two about stock cars."

The rear door locks clattered, and then the big rear panel began to power outward and down. The tall door was only halfway down when Trace saw the blue butt end of the Super Stock on the stacker level—and then a second, identical car on the bottom floor.

"Two cars!" Trace exclaimed.

"That's right, kid," Harlan said. "We got orders from headquarters to 'leave nothing to chance.' Exact words. So we built you two cars in case you wreck one right away."

"Gee, thanks," Trace said, with a sideways glance to his father.

Jimmy hooked up a braking cable, then an electric

motor whirred as the blue Super Stock rolled slowly backward, down its ramp, and into the sunlight. Trace stepped
forward.

"Whoa! Where are you going?" Harlan asked. He
blocked Trace's path.

"Uh, help with the car?" Trace asked.

"You drive the car. We load and unload it," Harlan said.
Trace stepped back.

"That's not us, that's orders from headquarters," Harlan
explained, bending to his work and with a glance to Tasha.

"Sorry," Tasha said to Trace. "That's all Laura. Corporate division-of-labor kinda thing."

Trace nodded, eyes on the car. A new race car—before
it got all banged up—was a beautiful thing. The blue tin
sides were as smooth as an airplane fuselage. The long, flat
deck lid flowed undented from the rear end, forward
around the cockpit, then past the upraised, round air
cleaner, and still forward to its downward tilt and the
Monte Carlo–style dirt nose. New dirt noses were themselves things of beauty: a down-force front end with facsimile headlamps embossed in the carbon fiber—and no
chips, tears, or blemishes.

Sweetness aside, Trace scanned the Super Stock body
design. No rear spoiler, no wheel skirts, no side skirts—
nothing obviously amiss. Trace worried that Super Stocks
from Tennessee were different from those in the Midwest;
car specs varied from sanctioning organization to sanctioning organization. He squatted down to check the
ground clearance.

"Four inches. Don't worry—the whole car was built to spec from your damned WISSOTA rule book," Harlan said.

Jimmy grinned and opened his mouth to say something.

"Just push the car, Son," Harlan said.

The car was so beautiful that Trace had no words. When the Super Stock was alongside the motor home, Harlan said to Jimmy, "That'll do."

Trace poked his head inside the cockpit. Everything was fresh and shiny: gauges, wheel, clutch, and gas pedal. Even the diamond-tread steel floor was unscuffed.

"Plenty of time to play with the car later," Harlan said. "Come on, I'll show you the hauler and your cabin."

Trace followed Harlan inside. Tasha brought up the rear. The tall trailer was a long, shiny-bright, square channel. At floor level, diamond-textured steel side compartments, a big tire's width wide, ran parallel along both sides. A car could sit nearly three feet off the floor—leaving plenty of room to work underneath it on a creeper. Harlan stopped to open the side compartment door labeled U-.

"U-joints, driveshaft and steering. U-bolts, drive and rear axle. Two new driveshafts. You break something on the drive train, we got two of everything," he said.

"We got more parts in this trailer than Speedway Motors!" Jimmy called.

The next steel cupboard was marked REAR END: drawers full of ring gears, pinions, splines, spools, carrier bearings, seals, gaskets, pinion nut washers, shims, O-rings, and more.

"Jimmy's your rear-end guy," Harlan said. "He can't read a road map, but he'll talk your head off about gear specs."

"It's just math, Pops," Jimmy said from behind as he retracted the cables.

Trace followed Harlan deeper into the trailer. Two unmarked drawers carried heavy padlocks.

"Them belong to Smoky," Harlan said. "He's got his stuff, we've got ours."

"He don't like anybody touching his stuff," Jimmy said.

Trace nodded.

"More rubber than you'll ever need," Harlan said, gesturing upward to a long rack of fresh-smelling tires that hung from the wall.

Trace loved the earthy, sweet smell of tire rubber. He touched the wide, pungent face on the nearest tire; its little rubber teats were springy and whiskery under his fingers.

"We'll see," Jimmy said. "Them Hoosiers is softer than Atlanta peaches."

"Once in a blue moon Jimmy is right," Harlan said. "I don't know why you're not running Goodyears up here."

The front end of the trailer was all shop, though it looked more like a hospital operating room. Stainless steel counters. Toolboxes as tall as Trace, including one with a steel cable locked tight across its face.

Trace glanced at Harlan.

"Smoky," he said.

On the left, strapped to the ends of a long tool bench, were two engines wrapped in plastic.

"He's got you a couple of fresh motors," Harlan said. "And this here electronic and dyno stuff is his, though he don't really use it much."

"So why did we buy it, then?" Tasha asked, an edge to her voice.

Harlan shrugged. "Oh, it will come in handy—don't get me wrong. If there's something we just can't figure out, he'll use it. But Smoky could build you an engine in the dark with a screwdriver and a pliers."

Trace gave his dad a look.

"And up here's your home sweet home," Harlan said, gesturing to the short flight of steps leading to a metal door. A curtained window looked into the interior of the trailer.

Trace walked up and opened the cabin door. Inside was an apartment, space-efficient like a motor home, but with everything: flat-screen television, couch, galley kitchen, microwave.

"Nice!" Tasha said. "Nicer than my apartment in Minneapolis."

"Bedroom's in the back," Harlan said. "Nice big bed—room enough for two." He winked broadly at Tasha.

Trace's face flushed, and he looked inside. Another, smaller television was built in over the bed.

"Nintendo, or whatever they call it nowadays," Harlan said, pointing toward the flat-screen. "Air-conditioning throughout, of course."

Trace and Tasha stepped back into the living room. He went to the little porthole-like window on the outside wall and pushed aside the curtain. The view was of the empty speedway, its shining metal bleachers.

"Your stuff is in the closet," Harlan said.

"My stuff?" Trace asked. He turned, then opened the little folding door. A new black Simpson racing suit hung from a hanger; on the shelf was a new top-of-the-line helmet plus gloves, booties, and neck collar.

"Should be the right size," Tasha said. "We ordered it straight off your poop sheet."

Outside, Jimmy fired the Super Stock's engine.

9

Trace quickly pulled on his new racing suit and shoes, then headed outside. Bonnet off, the big Chevy engine pulsed at a low growl. Jimmy sat in the cockpit looking at his cell phone. His gaze went to the dashboard gauges, then to his small, bright cell screen. Then back to the gauges.

Trace and his dad looked at each other.

Above the engine noise, Harlan said, "Jimmy's got a special cell phone diagnosticator, invented by yours truly. Picks up rpm, cfm flow in the carb, any valve issues, then relays that information back to the main computer on the mother ship."

Trace stared at Harlan—who busted up laughing.

"Had you goin' there, dint I?" he said. "He's just texting the figures."

Faint movement lifted Trace's eyes to the motor home. The sliding window was open a crack; centered in it was a knothole on a freshly peeled tree. Trace blinked. Actually, he was looking at an ear on the side of a man's bald head—except that the ear was gone. Left was a circle of fleshy bumps around a dark hole.

"That's Smoky," Harlan called as Jimmy blipped the accelerator. "Him and Jimmy got their own way of talking. Seems to work for them, so I stay out of it."

Trace's eyes stayed on Smoky's head. The ear hole angled slightly this way and that as it took in the engine sound. The rest of his skull was shiny and tight way beyond a close shave. There was no hair of any kind. Pink scars, like pale rose petals, drooped down on his neck.

Harlan looked toward the motor home window. "Smoky was a driver, but he had a bad wreck," Harlan said. "He crashed back before racetrack people really knew what they were doing when a car was upside down and on fire."

Trace looked at Harlan, then back to Smoky's shrunken knothole of an ear.

"You're lucky to be racing nowadays, kid," Harlan said, "though don't think it can't happen to you."

Inside the cockpit, Jimmy brought the rpm up to a steady, medium hum—then keyed in another text message. He waited, then nodded.

Harlan cupped his hands and shouted toward the motor home. "You like?"

A stubby, clawlike hand appeared. The pinkie finger

and one more were short a knuckle, but there were three good digits at least; the fingers formed a fist and half a thumbs-up sign, then withdrew. The window closed. Jimmy shut off the engine and got out. "All yours," he said to Trace.

The Kirkey full-containment race seat was softer and more form-fitting than any other Trace had sat in. The shoulder harness belts were wider and more comfortable across his shoulders. The sternum protector, a horizontal strap and buckle across the chest, was designed to hold the harness together under impact; it felt new and strange but that was not a bad thing—Trace had taken some hard hits in his old Street Stock. The new helmet felt stiff inside, but that would change. The visor, crystal clean and slightly tinted, was like a new pair of prescription glasses. He flexed his fingers (glad to have all of them) on the three-spoke aluminum steering wheel, then let his eyes traverse the cockpit.

The tinwork was perfect: metal corners at exact angles, rivets tight and flat, nothing sharp anywhere. The roll cage was sleeved with impact-absorbing flex-tubes— not the cheap, lightweight extruded-foam type on most amateur rides, but high-density rubber. The four-gauge panel was the top-of-the-line Auto Meter Ultra Nite: oil press, water temp, oil temp, fuel press.

"You do know how to operate one of these things, right?" Harlan asked.

Trace held up his hands as if completely baffled.

"Jeez," Harlan muttered to himself. "Listen up, then.

The transmission is internally clutched. That means you've got two speeds forward, and only one of them— first gear—is hooked into your clutch pedal. Once you're moving, you let off the clutch and push the shift lever into direct drive. You're good to go from there as long as you keep your rpm up. But remember, you gotta take it out of direct drive once you're in the pits. Otherwise, next time you hit the start button, you're gonna run over somebody."

Trace shifted easily in and out of first gear. "Kidding," he said to Harlan.

"Well, that's some consolation," Harlan replied. He stepped back and looked over the car. "You good to go?"

Trace nodded.

"Then what are you waiting for? Put a fire in the hole, kid!"

Trace eased in the clutch, then touched a finger to the rubber starter button. The engine caught on the first revolution, and the headers threw a steady, baritone rumble beneath the car. The sound waves vibrated upward through his seat, up his spine, and all the way into his teeth. Sitting in an idling Super Stock was like sitting on a rock-concert-size speaker with the bass notes pulsing through your butt. This motor had a deeper note even than Cal Hopkins's car.

"Drive it slow for about ten laps," Harlan called. "No more than 3000 rpm. We're breaking in the engine. This will give you some seat time."

"Will we get to some hot laps today?" Trace asked.

"Maybe, maybe not. There's no rush. We got all day here, and tomorrow, too, to get the car running right."

Trace saw his father glance at his watch, a frown flitting across his face.

"When's our first actual race?" Don asked.

Tasha spoke up. "That's up to Harlan, but if the car checks out, we'd like to debut Saturday night, Headwaters Speedway."

"Some rinky-dink track up north, I guess," Harlan added, with a wink to Tasha.

Trace pumped a gloved fist.

"Then Buffalo River, over by Fargo, on Sunday night," Harlan said. "Better get used to it, kid."

Trace spun the tires as he headed down pit row. There was nothing like the feeling of bridging up over pit lane and down onto a racetrack. A lumpy, banked oval of dirt, dry slick and dusty, or wet and muddy, never just right—but a place where you could drive as fast as you wanted to. As fast as you dared. There was no speed limit, no cops, no stoplights, no intersections, no dogs or deer or Sunday drivers to watch for. Stay on the track, stay right side up—those were the only things close to rules. Those and your arrangements with the turns. Each driver hammered out his own agreement with the four banked curves, the same as he did with the dirt itself. Racing was all and only about speed— what you and your car could handle. It was a team sport, but only up to a point. The team part ended when a driver steered his car out of the pits and down onto the track.

In the empty speedway, Trace eased the Super Stock slowly around the track. Weaving side to side, he tried to get a feel for the steering quickener, the tires, the weight distribution, the center of gravity. But he was tight in his arms and back. *Hold it loose and throw it hard.* He tried to relax and let the car do the driving, let it carry him around and around. Gradually his back muscles loosened and conformed to the seat. He started to feel the steering wheel, not choke it to death. After ten laps, he forgot and barked the engine once, breaking loose the tires; Harlan, standing at the pit entrance, immediately waved a rapid, palms-down warning.

"Oops." Trace backed off, and continued the slow crawl. Passing by the empty grandstand, he saw a man leaning on a broom; he was taking a break from sweeping to watch Trace pass. For an instant, Trace saw himself from the guy's eyes: a kid in a shiny blue, expensive race car rumbling by, a big hauler in the pit area, somebody from a different world.

After at least twenty laps, Harlan waved him in.

Trace braked beside the motor home; the window slid open a crack.

"Don't shut it down," Harlan called.

"I wasn't going to," Trace muttered.

Jimmy hustled to lift off the hood. Then, after looking at his cell screen, he made some carburetor adjustments. "Smoky says bring it up to 3000," Jimmy called.

Trace obeyed, eyes on the tach. It was odd how quickly he was getting used to this whole arrangement with Smoky the ghostly motor man.

"I'm not hearing it," Jimmy said, leaning closer to the engine. It was hard to tell if he was talking to himself or to Smoky.

"All right, got it," Jimmy added, and put the air cleaner back on.

"Let's do it again," Harlan said to Trace, jerking his head toward the track. "All seat time is good time. You can't rush getting right with a car. It's like building a house: you start from the bottom up, and it don't happen in one day."

To the side, Trace's dad and Tasha waited patiently. His dad sneaked another quick look at his wristwatch. Trace headed back onto the track. In the stands, the man with the broom was sweeping again; he did not look up as Trace passed.

The rest of the afternoon continued in this way, with Harlan and Jimmy making one small adjustment after another to the car. At three p.m., Trace got the green light for some medium-hot laps (5500 rpm maximum). The car flowed through the turns, a sweet, steady glide, but felt slightly heavy in the apex of the high banks.

Back in the pits, Trace said to Harlan, "It's pushing a little in the corners. My right front tire feels hard."

"I thought so, too," Harlan said. Jimmy was already scuttling around the car with a temperature gun. He pressed the handheld infrared thermometer on the treads of each tire.

"We're running fifty degrees hotter on the right front," he called to Harlan.

"Why don't you take a break?" Harlan said to Trace. "We got some work to do underneath this beast."

Like old times, Trace handed off his helmet to his dad, then pulled himself backward from the car.

"Listen," his dad began.

"You have to go," Trace finished for him.

His father gave Trace an apologetic look. "I've got a lot of stuff going on up north."

Stuff as in Linda, Trace wanted to say, but didn't. "That's cool," Trace said. "I'll be okay."

"You sure?"

"Hey, you saw my bachelor pad. It's not like I don't have a place to stay."

His dad nodded, but made no move to leave. He took a long look around, at the car, the motor home, the big hauler—then at Trace in his new black racing suit.

"You're not gonna get sand in your eyes again?" Trace said.

"Could happen," Don said, and swallowed.

"Well, don't let it," Trace said, and threw a quick hug on his dad. They walked over to the pickup, where Trace got his bag. "I'll see you up north." For some reason he didn't say "home."

"Call me when you get into town," his dad said quickly. Trace nodded.

"I'll remind him," Tasha said to Don.

Trace waved, as if to release his dad, to let him go.

Harlan's gaze followed Trace's dad as he walked slowly to his truck. "You see that, Jimmy?" he asked.

"What's that, Pops?" Jimmy scooted out from underneath the car on a creeper, and sat up to take a look.

Harlan pointed at Trace's dad, who by then was driving away.

"Some families know how to cut the cord," Harlan said. "It's a beautiful thing."

"What cord is that, Daddy?"

"See what I mean?" Harlan asked Trace.

Trace and Tasha ate ice cream at the Princeton Dairy Queen; then she was headed back to Minneapolis to report in to Laura and Team Blu.

"All good so far?" Trace asked.

"I'm not sure about the Smoky dude," Tasha said.

"Hey, the engine runs great!" Trace said.

"I guess that's the main thing," Tasha replied. "But what about Harlan and Jimmy? Can you deal with them?"

"Looks like I'll have to," Trace said.

"If Harlan gets to be too much, let me know and I'll have Laura yank his chain."

"I can take care of myself," Trace said. "But thanks."

They watched some teenagers come in, order at the counter—then break up with laughter over something one of them said.

"What?" Tasha asked.

"They're not that much younger than me," Trace said.

"So?"

Trace was silent. He looked back to his ice cream.

They continued to eat in silence. "So what about Mel?" Tasha asked at length. "How's that all going to work out?"

"It's not going to," Trace said.

Tasha nodded. She looked at him.

"What?" Trace asked, his turn this time.

"One of the reasons we chose you was that we thought you could deal with this whole thing better than most teenagers," she said. "You have sort of an old soul."

"Great," Trace said.

"No, that's a good thing!" Tasha laughed.

Trace was silent.

"Anyway, I still think you're the right one," she said, and patted his forearm.

"Thanks," Trace said. "Hey, what about that girl, Sara, from Fargo?"

"What about her?" Tasha said.

"Was she a finalist?"

"I really shouldn't say," Tasha said. "Let's put it this way: we liked her, but the marketing people liked you more."

"Do you have her address?" Trace asked.

"Why would you want that?" Tasha asked, teasing.

"Racing talk. That's all."

"Sure," Tasha said. "I do have her address, but I can't give it to you, sorry. I'm sure you understand."

She drove him back to the speedway, and in the parking lot they shook hands awkwardly. Then Trace gave her a hug. She felt good—strong and curvy—all over.

"No chicks in the trailer," she said, walking away. "I told Harlan to lock you down every night at ten o'clock."

"Thanks a lot!" Trace said. He watched her motor off in her little red Honda. She tooted the horn as she disappeared in traffic. Behind Trace, the Super Stock engine fired up.

Back on the track, Trace had the green light for more medium-hot laps. Not drop-the-green-flag hot laps, but the bring-it-up-slow kind. With late sun angling across the pit area and glinting in the aluminum bleachers, he gradually picked up his lap speed. All those endless, boring, slow laps were money in the bank; they were a driver's savings account—and now he was ready to spend some interest. Watching his tach, he powered harder and harder out of the turns. The blue car slung itself around the bank track, a roller-coaster car shooting a half-curl. Bleachers flashed by like they had at his tryout in Grand Forks—but he still had a quarter pedal and lots of rpm left. He was sweaty in his racing suit, but chilly goose bumps washed up his arms. This was a dream ride. The engine was something else. If they got the setup right, and if he drove it well, he could go all the way: win the Super Stock national points championship next year, eventually move up to sprint cars, maybe even—

By the pit entrance, Harlan waved him in. Trace blinked and lifted off the gas. He came in hot, and braked hard and on the money beside the motor home.

"Love it!" he called to Harlan.

"You'd better, kid," Harlan said as he leaned in to check the temperature gauges. Jimmy sprayed the radiator with water—which hissed and puffed white vapor like a steam iron.

The water temperature needle relaxed slowly backward. "Okay, shut her down," Harlan said, and withdrew his head from the cockpit.

Jimmy's phone beeped as Trace pulled himself from the car.

"Smoky wants us to drop that oil while it's still warm, and read the filter—see if there's any filings," Jimmy said.

"I doubt it," Trace said, peeling off his gloves. "The motor is something else. I had lots left out there."

"That's the idea," Harlan said.

"It's got all kinds of torque, it's quick, it breathes like crazy. The carb feels almost like a four-barrel," Trace said with enthusiasm.

Harlan paused to stare at Trace. The motor home window—though maybe it was Trace's imagination—eased slightly wider. "What did you say?"

Trace repeated himself.

Still nobody said anything.

"I mean, it's not a four-barrel, right?" Trace said quickly. "That would be against the rules. I just meant that it runs great."

Harlan glanced at Jimmy. "Take off that air cleaner," he said.

"Hey, I believe you," Trace said quickly.

"Seein' is believin'," Harlan said as Jimmy spun off the nuts. "Take a look for yourself."

Trace leaned over the carb.

"Does that look like a four-barrel?" Harlan said.

"No," Trace said quickly.

"What does it look like?"

"It looks like a regular Holley 500-cfm two-barrel," Trace said, an edge to his voice.

"There you go, then," Harlan said. He was not smiling, either. "I told you: we built this car according to your spec book."

"Okay, okay!" Trace answered. "I heard you the first time."

"Remember," Harlan said. "You drive. We take care of the car. Are we clear on that?"

Trace nodded, anger in his face.

"Good. Then that's it for today," Harlan said.

Trace stalked back to the trailer. Inside his room, he hung up his uniform and flipped on the television. After a hot shower, he lay back and watched the Speed Channel. Below, an electric motor hummed and the trailer rocked briefly as Harlan and Jimmy winched the Super Stock on board. Music, the Allman Brothers, began to play, punctuated by the occasional muffled clank of tools. Harlan and Jimmy talked, but kept their voices low. Trace could not make out what they were saying.

Some time later he started awake at a *tap-tapping* on his door. "Kid, you want some pizza?" Harlan called.

"Coming! Yeah," Trace called. Groggily he glanced at his watch; it was eight o'clock. He opened the door.

Harlan held some pizza boxes. "We called out. Not sure what you like, but here it is. Basic pepperoni."

"Thanks," Trace said. He took the top one.

"There's some cola in your fridge," Harlan said.

"Great," Trace said, still waking up.

"Catch you on the flip side," Harlan said. "More of the same tomorrow."

After Trace shut the door, he set his supper on the little table. Then he stepped to his side window and cracked the curtain. Harlan, carrying the other pizzas, was disappearing inside Smoky's motor home. The door closed behind him.

Trace ate a whole pizza, thin-crust, and gradually came alive. He called Mel, who did not pick up; he didn't leave a message—he was never any good at phone messages. After that he called his mother, who did not pick up, either.

"Hey, Mom. Dad and I met the crew and saw the car. Everything's cool. Love you." A generic message. No locations, no details, but a phone call nonetheless.

He called Patrick, who answered instantly. "Talk to me, dude!"

Trace smiled. "You ready to go racing Saturday night?"

"You know it," Patrick said.

"My dad is good with you in the Street Stock. You can use my suit and helmet. I'll help you get a driver's number from WISSOTA. Nothing to stop you after that," Trace said.

There was silence. Then Patrick said, "Awesome, man."

He didn't sound as surprised as Trace had expected. "Tell me about it. I'll be there, too, with my new car."

"Wow," Patrick said. "The local drivers are going to be so jealous, they'll pee their pants."

"I hope not," Trace said.

"Well, better get ready," Patrick said. "I mean, think about it. Guys like Gerry Harkness and the rest—they've been scraping along their whole lives, and now you show up with a full sponsor and a brand-new Super Stock."

"It'll give them something to talk about, I guess."

"I can't wait." Patrick giggled. "Thanks for talking to your dad, by the way."

"He thought it was a cool idea. Both of us can't wait to see you in yellow No. 32."

Patrick said, "Actually, your dad already called the speedway. Mel will let me take some practice laps tomorrow. She and Johnny will give me some pointers. Your dad's going to bring the car over himself."

It was Trace's turn to be silent.

"Hope you're all right with this," Patrick said. "I'm really pumped."

Trace paused. "Sure," he said finally. "I mean, it was my idea in the first place."

"Exactly what I told Mel," Patrick said quickly. "I knew you'd be cool with it."

There was a long moment of dead airspace. "Ever think you'd drive a race car?" Trace asked.

"To be honest, I'm sort of scared," Patrick said. "I

mean, not about getting hurt. I just don't want to wreck your car. I mean, it's not like I can afford to get it fixed."

"Don't worry about it. That car is already a wreck," Trace said.

"So far, nobody knows about this but you, your dad, Mel, Johnny, and Tyler."

"Hey, don't worry," Trace said. "If you're right about Saturday night, everybody will be so jealous of me that nobody will even notice you in the Street Stock."

Patrick laughed. They talked another couple of minutes about the car, though all Trace could think about was Mel and Patrick—and his dad, too—hanging out together in Trace's absence.

He made a couple more calls, hoping to get an incoming beep or at least a text message from Mel, but no luck. His last call was to his dad—who didn't pick up, either. Trace left a message. "Hey. Had a good rest of the day. More setup work tomorrow. See you soon."

Then he watched the Speed Channel until one a.m., when some motocross race came on. Motocross was not his thing. HBO had some cheesy late-night movie with middle-aged naked people, so he ended up watching a National Geographic special on lions. In the middle of a scene about a cute young female lion, Trace blinked and sat up. He went to his computer and keyed up racetracks around Fargo: Buffalo River, West Fargo, Ada, Grand Forks. It didn't take long to find her name: Sara Bishop. No address or e-mail, but that was a start. He killed the television, and lay back in bed imagining the two of them racing a Cruiser car, that novelty class just a notch above demolition derby beaters. In the same car, side by side, one person operated the gas pedal (a special setup) while the other person steered and braked. Crowds loved Cruiser races. And what a way to get to know someone, especially a racing girl.

Sometime later, Trace sat up in the dark. Inky, underwater darkness. A sharp *clack*—something had dropped—had awakened him. He thought for a moment he was in the motel in Eau Claire, but the sound in the room below was wrong—and now it was too quiet. Then he remembered where he was. He checked the green-glow numbers on his watch: 2:30 a.m. He lay back and listened. After a minute or two, faint sounds came from beneath him in the trailer: someone was working, and taking pains to be quiet about it.

Trace eased from bed and, without turning on his lights, held aside his curtain. Below, in the brightly lit trailer, a small man was bent over the Super Stock. He had on a Bardahl cap, the black, narrow kind that old-school mechanics wore, and wraparound dark safety glasses. He was taking off the carburetor. It was Smoky.

He held the carb up to the light. As he turned, Trace saw his face and nose—make that nose holes. Most of his nose was gone. Two black nostril openings hung just below his sunglasses like twin bullet-holes through a board. Rather than take off his dark glasses to see the carb better,

Smoky held the carburetor bowl up to his face. He sniffed deeply; he flicked the butterfly valves, letting their spring snap again and again. Then he set the carb aside and began to take off the manifold. His hands were faster on a wrench than Trace had ever seen.

After only a couple of minutes, Smoky stopped working. He looked over his shoulder at Trace's window. Caught, Trace kept the curtain open; he didn't want to act guilty. Smoky stared—then with a gnarled finger beckoned for Trace to come down.

Hurriedly Trace pulled on jeans and sweatshirt. He went down the metal stairs quietly.

Smoky waited for him, his face tight and shiny in the fluorescent lights. His nose holes pointed straight out. "Hello there," he said. His voice was soft and hoarse, as if the words came down a long, rusty pipe.

"Hello," Trace replied.

"I'm Bernard Lyle." Both of his hands contained tools, so there was no decision to make about a handshake.

"Trace Bonham."

"Some people call me Smoky, for obvious reasons."

Trace nodded. He was not sure what to say.

"I don't mean to be mysterious or frightening. I just have a problem with sunlight. I'm a little short on eyelids."

"You don't frighten me," Trace said.

"Good," Smoky said. He turned to look at the car. "What do you think?"

"It runs like a dream," Trace said quickly. "I can't wait until tomorrow."

Smoky's scarred lips widened in something like a smile. A crooked one.

"I love building engines," Trace said quickly. "I've got a lot of tech questions."

Smoky stared at him through his sunglasses.

Trace took that to be an invitation. He nodded at the Super Stock. "We can't do any polishing or grinding on either the heads or the intake manifold."

"That's right," Smoky said.

"But we can widen out the pushrod holes. We can grind the valve seats a quarter inch max, and we can balance the engine," Trace continued.

"Yes," Smoky said.

"But that's about it," Trace said in a rush. "We can't use anything aluminum, no aftermarket pistons or rods. We have to stick with 1.94 intake valves and 1.60 for exhaust. There's very little room to move. So how do you get an engine like this to run so good?"

Smoky pursed his scarred lips. "Go back to bed, kid."

"Huh?" Trace said.

"You leave the engine building to me. I'll do my job, you do yours. That way we'll get along just fine."

Trace stared. "Hey, I didn't mean anything."

Smoky pointed his wrench at Trace's cabin door.

"All right, all right," Trace said, backing away. He turned and headed up the stairs. From the top step, he turned and blurted, "I just like learning stuff, that's all."

10

Friday was another long day of testing and setup. Trace followed Harlan's orders without comment, doing exactly and only what he asked.

At noon, they sat in lawn chairs by the car and ate sub sandwiches. Nobody said anything. Harlan glanced at Trace. "You got a bee in your bonnet?"

Trace shrugged and kept eating.

"Smoky said you and him had a little conversation last night," Harlan said.

"If you can call it that," Trace said.

"Smoky's a crabby old fart," Harlan said loudly toward the motor home. "Don't take anything he says personal."

"I was just asking him some questions," Trace replied.

"Big mistake," Jimmy said softly. "He's kinda fussy about his engines. Got his own way of doing things."

"Hey, I like engines, too," Trace said. "I built my first Chevy motor when I was in seventh grade. It ran great. Still does."

Harlan opened his mouth, put a pinkie fingernail to something in his front teeth, then examined his find. "That's the sweet thing about racing," he said to no one in particular.

"What's that, Pops?" Jimmy asked.

"There's always something you hadn't planned on."

"Like what?" Jimmy asked.

"Mr. Mechanic, here." He nodded toward Trace. "I thought we was just getting a pretty boy who could drive—sort of. Now we got an engine builder, too."

Trace said nothing.

"Don't take that personal, either," Jimmy said to Trace. "Daddy's a crabby old fart, too."

Harlan narrowed his eyes as he looked at Trace. "Smoky has forgotten more about engines than the three of us will ever know."

"Guess he's a better engine builder than a driver," Trace said.

Jimmy looked quickly to his father; Harlan stared long at Trace. "Don't push it, kid, all right?"

Trace shrugged and went back to eating.

"And I was also going to say—before you got all bitchy—that you aren't the worst young driver I've ever seen," Harlan said.

"Gee, thanks," Trace said.

"Of course, we won't really know until we get some cars on the track," Harlan said. "It's easy to look good out there by yourself."

Saturday morning the Team Blu convoy rolled north on Highway 169. Trace sat up front to give directions. Since there was no rush—the pit gates at Headwaters Speedway didn't open until three p.m.—they stopped in Brainerd to check out North Central Speedway. The gates were locked, but Harlan, Jimmy, and Trace got out to stretch their legs and look around. Smoky opened his window almost halfway.

"Do speedways get any smaller?" Harlan said, shaking his head in astonishment.

"Actually, they do—by quite a bit," Trace answered.

"And you Yankees say the South is backward," Harlan threw back, shaking his head some more as he stared at an empty track and tin-sided grandstand.

They stopped to get a picture of Paul Bunyan and Babe the Blue Ox, then made a brief visit to Brainerd International Raceway, the National Hot Rod Association drag strip. Even Harlan seemed impressed. "Nice layout," he said, "but I've never understood drag racing. You work for days, for weeks on your car—and then the race is over in three or four seconds."

They rolled up Highway 371 through pine country and

small towns—far more pines than towns—as the blacktop curved this way and that.

"Can't they make the roads straight up here?" Harlan grumbled. "It's like the road builders were drunk."

"They had to go around the lakes, which are every-where," Trace said, pointing to some glinting water behind the trees. "And you know why that is?"

"No, why?" Jimmy asked.

"It goes back to Paul Bunyan," Trace said. And he told the legend of Babe the Blue Ox and his giant hooves, how they left gouges in the land that eventually filled up with water.

"Cool," Jimmy said, as if it might actually be true.

At the junction of Highways 371 and 200 sat the big Northern Lights Casino. As it came into sight, Jimmy's cell phone beeped. He looked at his text message.

"Smoky wants to stop and try his luck," Jimmy said to Harlan.

"I figured as much," Harlan said with a sigh.

"He's going to come out—in daylight?" Trace asked.

"He'd come out buck naked if that was the casino dress code. Smoky's a gambling fool."

Jimmy let out an annoyed sound. "Give him an hour, max. We got racing to do."

"We're ready to race," Harlan said as he eased the big rig to the far side of the casino parking lot. "You boys coming in?"

"Not me," Trace said. "You've got to be eighteen."

"Not me," Jimmy said. "Gambling is for people who are bad at math."

Harlan and Smoky headed across the parking lot to the casino, Smoky wearing a floppy hat and sunglasses. Trace headed to his cabin. "Want to come and hang out?" he asked Jimmy.

Jimmy shrugged. "No, thanks." Something else passed through his eyes, but didn't come out his mouth. "I think I'll just hang here and catch some NASCAR on my little TV."

"I'm only gonna relax and do some e-mail. You can watch on my flat-screen."

"No, thanks," Jimmy said again.

Trace paused a moment, then shrugged, and passed through the door to his cabin.

He called his dad, who was on his way back from northwestern Minnesota—the wheat harvest was still going full-bore. "I'll be there for the feature," he said. "I can't wait to see you—and Patrick."

"Yeah," Trace said flatly.

"And I have to ask," his dad said. "Would you mind if I brought Linda? She'd like to meet you."

Trace was silent. "It's a free country," he replied.

"Thanks, Son," his father said quickly—clearly not picking up on Trace's tone. "See you at the track."

Trace called Patrick, who was all set to race. "What if I throw up in your car?" he asked.

"We—you—hose it out," Trace said.

And Mel actually picked up. "Hey, big-shot stranger," she said before he could speak.

"Yeah, well, at least I return calls."

"Sorry. I've been up to my eyeballs in track stuff. Talking with bankers, with other speedways, with the World of Outlaws people. It could really happen next summer, Trace!" she said. "Sprint cars back at Headwaters. I get goose bumps just thinking about it."

"Wow," Trace said.

"My plan is to start with a special event night. Then we'll try to get some of those Fargo independent sprint car drivers over here once a month. Donny Schatz said he'd make some calls and do what he could."

"You actually talked to Donny Schatz?"

"Sure," Mel said.

"No wonder you didn't return my call."

Mel laughed. "Once you get your name on a racing T-shirt, maybe I will."

"Speaking of racing, guess what? I'm coming home tonight with my new car."

There was a pause. "Um . . . Patrick already told me," Mel said.

It was Trace's turn to pause. "Well, isn't that nice?" he said.

"Hey, he's excited for you—me, too."

"Really?"

"Yes. And it should be a big night. It's two thousand to win, and we're expecting lots of cars," Mel said.

"Two thousand to win!" Trace exclaimed.

"I've been advertising heavily, especially in Fargo and Grand Forks," Mel continued. "There are lots of Super Stocks over that way, and a bigger purse is the only way we're going to get those cars here. When they see my plans for the speedway next summer, they'll come back—that's the idea anyway."

"So what are your ideas for tonight?" Trace asked.

"Smooth—very smooth," Mel said. "What did I tell you about race car drivers?"

"No, it's not that," Trace said immediately.

She laughed briefly. "Tonight? Tonight's gonna be busy and then some."

"I want to show you the car, the hauler, my cabin," Trace said. "It's amazing."

"A good girl never goes inside a race car hauler or a rock star's motor home," Mel said, a smile in her voice. "But I'll try to come by and take a peek."

"Great!" Trace said—a bit too enthusiastically.

"Hey, incoming. Looks like a banker. I gotta go," Mel said.

"See you—" Trace answered, but she was already gone.

Harlan and Smoky came back almost two hours later. Trace started awake as Harlan slammed the door, then sat down heavily in the driver's seat. Trace poked his head into the cab.

"Don't ask," Jimmy said, putting a finger to his lips.

"I don't know how he does it," Harlan said as he threw the truck in gear. "You should see him. He drifts around the dollar slot machines until he finds 'the one.' It's like he listens to them."

Waiting for Harlan to lead him out, Smoky tooted his motor home horn as if excited to get on the road.

Trace guided Harlan up to Highway 2, then west a few miles. "This is the Leech Lake Indian Reservation," Trace said.

"They thank you for leaving them your money," Jimmy added.

"Dry up," Harlan threw back.

"Turn north here," Trace said, pointing.

"Uh-oh!" Harlan said. He looked up at the big Palace Casino sign.

Jimmy's cell phone beeped.

"Don't answer that," Harlan said, and picked up speed.

They passed the second casino without losing Smoky, and wound around lakes and over bridges. "Seems like we're going in circles," Harlan said. "We keep crossing the Mississippi River."

"That can't be the Mississippi," Jimmy said, staring out his window.

"Sure it is," Trace said.

"I could throw a rock across."

"You could drink out of it, too, and it wouldn't kill you," Trace said. The river, shallow and clear, with green shoulders of wild rice, curved out of sight into the woods.

"That *can't* be the Mississippi," Jimmy said again.

"Keep going," Trace said to Harlan. "Another couple of miles and we'll turn left." He was excited to be home.

Ahead, a rusted pickup pulling a homemade trailer and battered Pure Stock turned in front of them. The driver slowed to stare at the Team Blu convoy. "That's gotta be our road," Harlan said, gearing down. He followed the Pure Stock.

Trace leaned forward in his seat, eager to see his track. Only another half mile. "Here we are!" he said.

"Where?" Harlan asked.

"Headwaters Speedway."

Harlan and Jimmy stared. Behind them, in the mirror, Smoky's motor home had dropped back several lengths as if Smoky was lost or confused.

"You got to be kidding," Harlan said.

"Nope," Trace said. "This is it."

11

Harlan eased the Team Blu rig down the bumpy gravel driveway and past the grandstand. "Wooden bleachers," he said.

"It's like out of some old movie," Jimmy added. His mouth hung open.

A few early-bird fans stopped to stare at the big blue rig.

"Up ahead is the pit gate," Trace said, pointing to the little open-fronted shack. When Harlan stopped, Trace swung down to the ground.

"Trace!" called Rebecca, one of the gate girls. "It's true!" She looked in awe at the towering Freightliner tractor and trailer.

"Guess so," Trace said.

Harlan and Jimmy came up to the counter. "The Blu crew," Trace said, and made introductions; he was not yet ready to say "My crew."

Harlan looked across at the speedway to the pits behind. "This is it?" he asked.

"Excuse me?" Rebecca asked. She smiled in that Minnesota-nice way.

"This is the whole speedway?"

Rebecca's smile faded slightly. "That's right."

"I thought Mr. Driver here was pulling my leg," Harlan said.

The other pit gate girl held out the pouch for Trace to draw.

"What's this?" Harlan asked.

"It's how we draw here," Trace said. He picked a chip: number 97. Not a good sign.

"No computer draw?" Jimmy asked; he was more surprised than sarcastic.

"For that you'd have to have electricity," Harlan said under his breath.

"Pit passes are twenty bucks," said Rebecca; she was no longer smiling.

Harlan laughed for real this time.

"Is there something wrong?" Rebecca asked.

"No. Twenty bucks is the only right thing I've seen so far," Harlan said, dropping a credit card on the plank counter.

"We don't take credit cards," Rebecca said.

After paying cash to sign in the team, Harlan drove

along pit row, which curved around homemade concrete squares fronted by scarred log-skidder tires. Weeds grew up around the tires. Arriving with strangers, Trace saw it through a stranger's eyes. Parts of the back pit area, with old wreckers and busted-up water tanks, looked more like the back lot of an old World War II movie. The grandstand tilted slightly to the west, something he had never noticed before. People in the bleachers made adjustments with seat cushions and blankets in order to sit up straight—and no one ever complained.

In the Pure Stock pit area, Leonard, the basketball player who helped crew for Sonny Down Wind, was changing a tire on the red and black No. 66. He paused to stare, his hands horizontal on the lug wrench. Two other crews from the reservation swiveled their heads, their long black ponytails catching sunlight.

"We're not in Kansas anymore," said Jimmy, looking at the crews and their beat-up cars.

"Or maybe we are," Harlan said.

"See that guy there?" Trace said, pointing. "That's Sonny Down Wind. If his last name had been Allison or Unser or Petty, you'd be watching him race on television."

"Do they have television up here?" Harlan asked. He made a wide swing, then pulled up next to the pit bleachers, where the Bialacheks always parked.

"This spot is reserved for another crew," Trace said.

Harlan looked again through the windshield. "I don't see any 'reserved' signs."

"It's sort of understood," Trace explained. "The regular racers all have their slots."

"If there aren't any signs, it's first come, first served," Harlan said, braking. "Besides, we need a place where Smoky can see the track and hear the car."

"I don't want to piss everybody off my first time back," Trace said.

"You drive the car, remember?" Harlan said, setting the air brakes. "We'll take care of the pissing-people-off part."

"Well, you're off to a damn good start," Trace replied. He got out, slammed the door, and stalked away. Barely three days with Harlan felt like a whole racing season—which was also not a good sign. Just then the Harkness family and their old school-bus hauler, driven by Cindy, motored along the pits.

"Hey, kid!" Gerry called from his open window.

"Hey, boss!" Trace replied. Cindy turned in to their usual slot alongside Trace's old space.

Gerry quickly got out and dropped to the ground. "That your rig?" he said, nodding to the blue hauler.

"That's me."

"The Bialacheks ain't gonna be happy," Cindy said as she and Tim climbed out.

Trace shrugged. "I tried," he said, not wanting to go into it.

"That is *some* rig," Gerry said, still staring.

"Wow," whispered Tim.

Even Cindy seemed impressed.

Jimmy had already powered down the back gate; Harlan stood nearby, watching his every move.

"Well, what are we waiting for?" Gerry said, clapping a big hand against Trace's back. "Show me around!"

They all headed to the blue trailer, pausing to watch as Jimmy winched the shiny Super Stock down the ramp and onto the dusty grass.

"Holy smokes, that's a pretty one!" Gerry said to Harlan and Jimmy.

They said nothing. They kept working.

Trace had planned to make introductions, but then decided against it.

"Brand-new!" Gerry added.

"Yup," Jimmy said, with a glance to his dad.

"Well hey, congratulations again," Gerry said to Trace. "How about a look inside?" He stepped forward onto the trailer's ramp.

"Excuse me!" Harlan said, and moved to block Gerry's way.

Gerry stared. "Say what?"

"This is a private hauler," Harlan said. "It's off-limits to the public. We have a lot of expensive equipment in there, plus there are liability and insurance issues."

Gerry looked confused. " 'The public'?" he asked. "I'm not 'the public.' I race here every Saturday night—have for twenty years."

"Come on," Cindy said, tugging her husband's arm. He shrugged off her hand.

"That's us over there," Tim said helpfully, and pointed.

Harlan looked across at the old school-bus hauler and Gerry's battered Super Stock. He laughed, a deep, belly laugh. "Look at that hauler, Jimmy. They should call this place the Flintstone Speedway."

Tim frowned, then his face bunched into a hurt look. Cindy yanked him away, and marched him by the arm back across the pit road. Gerry remained; a vein started to pulse on his forehead.

"Look here," he began.

"Get off our ramp," Harlan said. "We got work to do."

Gerry bit his lip, then stepped back. He turned to Trace. He gave him a long stare. "What the heck have you gotten yourself into?" he asked.

Word traveled fast; no more locals approached the trailer. Trace sat alone by the car making calls. Harlan and Jimmy were out walking the track, inspecting the corners. And where was Mel? Why hadn't she at least called? Where were Patrick and Tyler with Trace's yellow No. 32? And his father and Linda—he had almost forgotten about that.

Harlan and Jimmy came back shaking their heads. "Where's the clay?"

"Say what?" Trace replied.

"Somebody steal it?" Jimmy asked.

"That's bedrock and gravel out there," Harlan said. "Stones the size of watermelons."

"The big ones don't come up—usually," Trace said.

"I sure hope they don't," Harlan said.

Another Super Stock rig came slowly along the pits. It

was nothing fancy. A dusty crew-cab Dodge truck pulled a homemade trailer with a rough-looking Super Stock chained and swaying on top. Its sides were more wrinkled than a turkey's neck, but they were freshly painted. Fluorescent red and orange lettering read BISHOP PLUMBING & HEATING, FARGO, NORTH DAKOTA. A teenage girl with short hair, and wearing sunglasses, sat in the rider's seat. He looked closer; she turned her head to stare at him. "Hey!" she called, and lifted her chin.

"Hi, Sara," he called back.

She turned and said something to the driver—clearly her dad, as they both had the same pug nose. The pickup braked.

Trace walked over.

"So is this it?" she asked, looking behind Trace at the big blue hauler. "Team Blu?"

"Hard to miss," he said.

"That's the purpose, I suppose," she said. "Congrats! I figured it would be you."

Trace didn't know what to say: "Sorry you didn't get the ride"?

"So where do new people park around here?" she asked.

"Take my old spot," Trace said, pointing. "It even has a couple of trees for shade."

"Thanks!" she said. Her freckles had darkened, which made her smile all the brighter. She was cuter than he remembered.

"How did you do on the draw?" Trace asked.

"Number 4."

"Excellent," Trace said.

"How about you?"

"I'll be watching you from way back."

"Hope you stay there," Sara replied with a grin, and motioned her father forward.

"Way back" was all the way back. Trace's draw, when the heat lineups were finally listed, put him in the last row, outside, in the last heat. And Mel was right: there were lots of Super Stocks—more than Trace had ever seen at Headwaters. By five o'clock they still trickled in. The chance for national WISSOTA points plus two thousand dollars had clearly broken loose cars from their home speedways, and sent them on the road to Headwaters.

The pit boss came by on his ATV. "Packing!" he said, and gestured at Trace and the blue Super Stock.

"Packing?" Harlan said from the mouth of the trailer.

"Track has been watered," the official said. "We need all the big cars out there to get the mud firmed up."

"This is a new Super Stock, it's not a damn tractor," Harlan said.

The pit boss stared, then said, "Suit yourself." He drove on.

Trace ran his fingers through his hair and let out a long sigh.

Mel finally came zipping up on Johnny's ATV. In shorts, her legs were long and tanned, as were her arms.

"Well, well, well," she observed, looking at the big blue hauler.

"You like?" Trace asked.

She tilted her head this way and that as she stared. Her eyes fell to Harlan and Jimmy. "I already don't like your crew. The pit gate girls are not happy."

"Sorry about that," Trace began.

"Neither are the Bialacheks," Mel said. "They had to park way down by the fence."

"I tried," Trace said again, and left it at that.

"Anyway, the pit girls said it wasn't you," she said with a shrug.

"Come by later?" Trace said.

She paused a moment. "I'll try," she said, and accelerated down pit row.

At long last Patrick appeared, riding with Tyler as they pulled Trace's Street Stock on his old trailer. Trace waved them forward alongside the Bishop family's Super Stock; there was just enough room.

"About time!" Trace called. "I thought you chickened out."

Patrick managed a tiny smile. He looked scared.

"You missed the draw," Trace said.

"He's starting in back, anyway," Tyler said, "so I didn't think it mattered."

"Good point," Trace said.

"Plus I couldn't get off work early," Tyler said. "Some of us have real jobs."

"Hey, no problem. This is just for fun," Trace said.

"Sure," Tyler said. He stared across at the big blue hauler. "Is that you?"

"That's me," Trace said.

"Jeez," Patrick said with admiration. Tyler didn't say anything at all.

"Hey, Trace. You driving in two classes tonight?" Gerry asked from the side.

"Nope," Trace said, as he helped Tyler unload the car.

Gerry walked over, scratching his head. He looked at Tyler, then at Patrick.

"He's driving," Tyler said, nodding to Patrick.

Trace winced; the idea was to keep this on the down-low.

"Yeah, right," Gerry said with a big laugh. He muscled Patrick into a brief headlock for a knuckle rub. "This kid? The one with the golden pipes? Him drive a race car? That'll be the day."

"Guys in the NBA have rap albums out," Patrick said, extricating himself. "Nobody tells them they can't play ball and sing."

"That ain't singing, and you're not seven feet tall," Gerry said.

As Gerry walked away chuckling, Patrick shot him a steely glare and muttered a few words that Trace had never heard him use.

While they readied the Street Stock, Patrick sat in the driver's seat taking deep breaths. "So I won't hyperventilate during the race," he explained.

"You'll be fine," Trace said. "And good luck out there."
To give Patrick some space, he strolled over to Sara's car.
The red and orange No. 17 was an older Super Stock, but
well taken care of under the bonnet. The valve covers were
mirror-shiny; the engine sounded loud, smooth, and on
the money.

"This is my dad," Sara called over the noise, and made
the introductions.

"Hi there," her father said. He had rough, thick fingers, but an open, honest smile—like Sara.

"Saw you over at Grand Forks," Trace said.

"That's quite a deal you landed," her father said, looking across at the blue hauler.

"Thanks. We'll see how it goes," Trace said. He turned
to Sara. "I'll show you around the track if you want."

She looked at her father.

"Go ahead, we're pretty much ready," he said. He bent
back over the engine compartment and tweaked the
throttle one more time.

As they walked along pit row, Trace pointed. "There's
where you get racing fuel if you need some. That's the tech
lane. Top five finishers have to stop there after the feature."

"Same as my speedway," she said, "not that I've been
teched for a while."

Trace glanced sideways at her. She had a great personality, the kind that stretched all the way from her brain to
the bottoms of her red, soft-soled racing shoes. "Hey, I
saw you drive," he said. "This could be your night."

"Not with Team Blu here," she answered. "I hear they've got this great young driver."

"He's probably way overrated," Trace said.

They stopped by Amber Jenkins's Mod-Four. Trace introduced the girls, who hit it off immediately and exchanged cell phone numbers.

"I'm surprised at the number of girl drivers here," Sara said as they walked on.

"Girl drivers are a good thing," Trace said.

"There must be a shortage of decent guys around here," Sara continued. "Instead of dating, the girls go racing on Saturday night."

"Very funny," Trace said.

Sara laughed. Trace glanced toward the announcer's booth; because of the tinted glass, he could never tell where Mel was, or what she might be seeing.

At the drivers' meeting, the chief pit steward read the rules. Then he said, "Some of you didn't help pack the track, so you start at the rear. That includes No. 32 in the Street Stock, and 18x in the Super Stock."

"Fine by me," Harlan muttered to Jimmy. "We won't be in the back very long."

A couple of nearby drivers glanced at Harlan, then Trace.

After the meeting, and the national anthem (a recording tonight), a small field of Mini-Stocks ran their heats. Then came the Street Stocks.

Trace walked quickly back to Sara's car. "You gotta

watch this," he said to her, and explained the deal with Patrick.

"Fun!" she said, and joined him on the small section of pit bleachers.

Trace's phone beeped twice. WISH US LUCK read the text message from Mel.

Us. Trace glanced toward the tinted windows of the announcer's booth, then concentrated on the track. It was really strange seeing his yellow No. 32 come slowly by— one more out-of-body experience tonight. Patrick sat ramrod straight in the seat; there was a hand's width of airspace between his back and the seat pad.

"Relax!" Trace shouted. "Bend your arms or you'll break them!" Calling instructions against the rumble of ten Street Stock engines was useless, of course, but everybody did it.

On the second slow lap, as the cars found their positions, Patrick settled back in the seat a bit. Following the drivers ahead, he swerved the car left and right.

"Yeah, that's it!" Tyler shouted. He, too, was getting into it.

At the green flag, the cars surged forward. Trace's yellow No. 32 hesitated, then cautiously followed the pack. Patrick took a high line, where he could stay out of trouble—a good move, because the lead cars mixed it up right away in turn 2, breaking a wheel off one car and bringing out a yellow flag.

On the restart, another Street Stock came up limping

—something wrong with the front suspension—and gradually dropped back. When Patrick passed the slower car, Trace and his group went crazy.

Getting by his first car clearly gave Patrick a huge rush. He suddenly picked up the pace, took a lower line, and brought Trace's car up tight against the end of the pack.

"Oh yeah!" Trace shouted.

"That's it!" Sara called.

When two cars just in front of him bumped and rocked each other in a grudge match, Patrick dove low and picked them off.

Trace and his friends cheered, as did Gerry Harkness, who had come over to see what the fuss was about. "I don't believe it!" Gerry said.

"Believe it," Trace shouted.

Some races were not winnable; other races belonged to a driver from the moment the green flag dropped. This Street Stock heat fell somewhere in between. Patrick, with the help of several restarts, found himself running third with four laps to go. When Sonny Down Wind blew a radiator hose and went up in steam, Patrick slid into second place and hung there. Trace and the crowd of pit fans went wild.

On the white-flag lap, Patrick threw the yellow No. 32 into the turns like a maniac—way too deep, way too much brake—but he spewed dirt from the rear tires as he thundered out of the high banks and down the straightaway. Trace stopped cheering. His jaw dropped, and the cars

went by in slow motion on the last lap—with Patrick winning the heat by a car length.

Art Lempola, the announcer, rattled the mic—fumbled for several seconds—then said, "Ladies and Gentle-
men, we have a driver correction on No. 32. In Trace
Bonham's No. 32 Street Stock we have a special guest
driver tonight—Patrick Fletcher!"

The crowd cheered and thundered the pine boards.

Trace waved frantically for Patrick to pull in. He
roared up to the pits entrance—where Trace blocked his
way.

"Seven feet tall!" Patrick shouted, and pumped his fist.
"Where's Gerry now?"

"Forget about Gerry. You have to go back—across the
scales—for it to be official!" Trace shouted.

Patrick blinked.

"And then get your picture taken with the checkered
flag," Trace said.

"Oh God," Patrick said. "I didn't think about that!"

The WISSOTA pit boss glanced questioningly at Trace
and Patrick. As he raised his arm to disqualify No. 32,
Patrick spun the tires, yanked the steering wheel, and
headed to the scales. Smiling, Trace watched Patrick have
his picture taken. Heat winners stayed inside their cars,
and held up the checkered flag. Patrick kept his helmet on.

After he suited up, Trace went to the fence to catch
the Mod-Four heats (Amber ran away with hers).

"You gonna race tonight or not?" Harlan asked behind
him.

"Coming," Trace said, and headed back to Team Blu.

As a team, they watched the first two Super Stock heats. Harlan jotted down notes. Jimmy kept his binoculars on the cars, the turns, the dirt itself. Smoky sent continual text messages, most of which Jimmy replied to.

"Smoke says there's some decent cars out there," Jimmy said.

"For Flintstone Speedway," Trace added for Harlan's benefit.

"You just get out there and show them what a real car can do," Harlan said.

Rolling down onto his old track in the new Super Stock was more than a little strange. Trace kept reaching for things—shifter, clutch—with muscle memory left over from his Street Stock. Way ahead was the slow-swerving tail end of Sara Bishop's red and orange No. 17. The Bialachek No. 28 was fifth row outside; Trace expected to see more of that car, close-up, before the night was over. He blipped the throttle again and again to make sure the engine was loose; the tires broke free each time in a spray of brown dirt. In truth, Harlan was right: the clay was mostly gone here, thrown up over the ends, or else carried into pit row and scraped off the race cars. Art Lempola's excited voice played inside his helmet like a faint and far-off radio station—and then the Super Stocks surged forward toward the green.

Trace was in no hurry. He knew he had plenty of

power, so he let the heat race come to him. The turns at Headwaters were basically two-wide, and it was difficult to slip between bunched-up cars; however, the straightaways belonged to Trace. By lap 5 or so, when the cars began to string out, Trace went on the hunt. He powered ever faster through the turns, then pulled the other Super Stocks, one by one, down the straights. Bialachek seemed to feel Trace coming, and swerved to box him out; Trace tucked against his tail, then took him high on the outside. He passed Bialachek as if No. 28 had slipped out of gear. "Yeah, baby!" Trace shouted.

Heat races were short, so he kept pressing. Sara was running second when he came up behind her. She had the inside line in turn 2, so he tried another outside sweep. She responded by laying her right front corner against Trace's driver's side—*boom!* Trace fought the wheel as he slid way high, almost to the rim; overcorrecting, he dove back down, into the infield, swerved between two big bumper tires in an explosion of dust, and was quickly back on Sara's tail—where he stayed to finish third in the heat.

In the pits, Trace pulled himself out as Harlan knelt beside the bashed-in blue tin. Trace glanced over at Sara, who only smiled and turned away.

"Was that a girl who did that?" Harlan asked, touching the tin. "Tell me it ain't so."

"Girls up here are well above average," Trace said.

"I guess!" Jimmy said, admiration in his voice.

Gerry walked over, though only partway. He beckoned to Trace, who met him in the middle of pit row.

Gerry had an odd look on his face. He lowered his voice. "What's with that engine?"

"What do you mean?" Trace asked. Any fun he was having tonight evaporated, blew away like a tear-off sucked through a stock car's window.

"It's pretty fast," Gerry said.

Trace shrugged. "It's a professionally built engine," he said. "I just drive the car." His adrenaline was still up after driving; racing brought out the fight in anyone.

Gerry pursed his lips, then walked away.

"What was that all about?" Harlan asked when Trace returned.

"I don't know," Trace said. But he probably did know: it was the whole sponsor thing. Patrick had called it after all.

The evening went downhill from there. As if clouds and a cold front had moved in, his father showed up with Linda. She was overly cheerful, had big hair, and was curvy—all the things Trace's mother was not. They made small talk, and then Trace excused himself to "get ready."

"We'll be over in the grandstand," his father said. He gave Trace a clumsy hug.

Linda gave him one, too; she had on perfume. "Good luck, kiddo!" she said with a wink.

"Thanks," Trace said curtly, and turned to his car. He looked over his shoulder as they walked away—just in time to see his dad pat Linda on her butt.

Trace watched the Pure Stock and Mod-Four feature by himself. Patrick finished in the number 12 spot, decent among the nineteen-car field; Sonny Down Wind came from the rear to finish second. Amber placed third in the Mod-Fours—and suddenly it was time for the Super Stock feature.

Trace rolled down onto the track angry. Something dark and hard and brittle—a whole bunch of built-up stuff—let loose inside him. Starting in the fifth row outside (there were twenty-six cars), he hammered down at the green and picked off three cars before turn 1. He drove hard and angry. By lap 5 he was running eighth, and by lap 10 he was in fourth place—which was when Bialachek and Gerry Harkness boxed Trace in. As he tried to slice between them, the two veterans pinched Trace. Tin shrieked. His car bucked and rocked over somebody's front tire—and he spun backward up and over the rim of the turn. After a brief—but very long—moment of hang time, his car slammed down hard on the far embankment and stalled in an explosion of dust. Trace pounded his palms on the wheel and swore.

A push truck came speeding over, along with two track guys on ATVs. They jumped off and inspected the tin and the undercarriage—then gave Trace a thumbs-up. Trace fired the engine, and waved off the truck. Back on the track, Sara's red and orange Super Stock sat tilted with a damaged right clip; the front tire leaned sideways like a bird with a broken wing. A wrecker backed toward her, cable hook swaying. Trace held up his hands apologetically; Sara nodded and gave him a what-can-you-do? wave.

Lining up for the restart before a held yellow flag, cars

nosed forward toward the slots that the drivers believed they deserved. This was the drama that grassroots race fans loved: who was to blame for the yellow flag? Trace idled forward near the front—the spinout was certainly not his fault—then waited as car after car was waved ahead of him. The chief pit steward finally pointed his furled yellow flag at Trace to bring up the rear.

Trace's anger surged back. He forgot about Sara, and on the restart he drove as much to punish as to win. Streaming by up high on the marbles, he knifed down through the turns, knowing a space would open for him—and it did every time. By lap 17 of the twenty-five-lap feature, he was pulling every car he came up behind. Nobody had horsepower, nobody had torque like the blue No. 18x. By lap 22, he was back up front—not all the way, but in the third slot.

Gerry Harkness, who had kept his nose clean, tried to block Trace up high. Trace streamed by him on the inside, making Gerry's car look like a Street Stock. Trace could have tried for first, and risked a spinout, but he got a grip on himself and settled for second place behind a veteran driver from Winnipeg.

After the weigh-in, Trace headed off the track. At the pit entrance, two stewards in safety vests jerked their yellow flags at him and pointed to the tech lane.

"I know, I know," Trace muttered. He waited in line, his engine still hot, behind the winning car. Its tech check took about a minute: bonnet off, a quick look at the carb, manifold, and exhaust headers, then out the other side and back home to its trailer.

Trace pulled forward. The pit boss leaned into his car. "You might as well shut it down and get out," he said. "This is gonna take a while."

"Have at it," Trace said. He jerked off his helmet. By then Harlan and Jimmy had arrived.

"You got some problem with our car?" Harlan said.

"Step back and shut up," the pit boss said to them, "or your driver gets a DQ right now."

Trace scrambled out of the car, his anger still flowing in him like a black river.

Harlan stepped between Trace and the pit boss. "Walk back to the trailer; we'll take care of this," he said.

Trace glared, then turned away.

In his cabin he peeled off his uniform, then stashed his helmet and gloves and shoes. He sat down—tried to calm himself. He leaned back and drank a full bottle of water. Then, below, he heard someone calling his name. He jerked open his cabin door. "What?" he said, anger still in his voice.

"You are here!" Sara said. "Sorry. I just wanted to say congrats."

"Hey, wait," Trace said quickly. He hurried down the cabin steps, catching up with her before she left the trailer. "Sorry you wrecked."

"That's racing," she said.

They looked at each other; both had sweaty faces and damp hair.

"That was some driving," she added. "I see now why they picked you."

Trace felt himself coming down. On the track, it was like he had turned into someone else. "I don't know what happened. I was sort of insane out there, actually," he said.

"Maybe that's what it takes," Sara said. "Anyway, you're gonna do great. Promise you won't forget us little people when you get famous?"

Trace smiled. "As if that's going to happen."

They hugged each other—a brief, all-good hug between friends. Trace felt himself come full back into his own body, into his own brain—which was a really nice feeling. So nice it made him hang on to Sara an extra second. In the middle of that long moment, Trace looked over Sara's shoulder and saw Mel standing in silhouette at the end of the trailer, watching.

12

Harlan and Jimmy returned without the car. Trace heard them coming along the side of the trailer, laughing. Harlan pulled up at the sight of Trace sitting alone inside the long trailer. "There's this old joke," he said. "A horse walks into a bar. 'Hey, buddy,' the bartender says, 'why the long face?' "

Nobody laughed.

"You done good out there," Harlan said to Trace. "Even Smoky said so, right, Jimmy?"

Jimmy held up his cell phone.

"Where's the car?" Trace said.

"Those green-jacket boys are crawling over it like hornets on a dead horse," Harlan replied.

At that moment, Trace's dad and Linda appeared.

"Great driving, Son!" his dad called. Trace stepped out to meet them.

"Wow!" Linda said to Trace. "I had no idea."

"Patrick did fine, too," Don said with a broad smile. "I think he should drive your car next year."

Trace paused. "Sure. Why not?"

"Looks like the tech boys don't like your car," Don said, turning to Harlan.

"Don't worry, they won't find anything," he said.

"That's good to know," Trace's dad said. Linda kept smiling at Trace.

Johnny Walters rode up fast on his ATV, the pit boss perched behind him. "Trace, we need to talk to you," Johnny said. He nodded briefly to Don.

"We'd better go, honey," Linda said to Trace's dad. "Trace looks like a busy boy."

"Call me," his dad said to Trace. He and Linda walked off hand in hand.

Trace turned to Johnny and the pit boss.

"I have good news and bad news," the man said. "We don't like what we saw, but on the initial inspection, our tech guys didn't find anything wrong."

"I could have told you that," Harlan said.

The pit boss ignored Harlan. "The bad news is—your engine has been protested. More than one driver thinks you've got a cheater engine, and one of them has made a formal protest."

"Who?" Trace asked, his anger swelling up again.

"Me," said Gerry Harkness from the shadows. He

stepped forward into the trailer lights. "That engine ain't kosher. No way!"

"Mr. Harkness has put down a two-hundred-dollar protest fee," the pit boss said.

"Top- *and* bottom-end inspection," Gerry said. "Then we'll see what's what." There was nothing friendly about him anymore.

"You have the right to refuse a teardown," the pit boss continued. "But if you do, you forfeit all winnings and points for this event, and you incur a loss of all national points to date, a thousand-dollar fine, and a thirty-day suspension."

"Or, if everything is kosher, we make money, right?" Harlan asked.

"Correct," Johnny said. "Of the protest fee, fifty dollars would go to the track, and a hundred and fifty dollars to your team."

"That's gas and pizza money," Harlan said. "Have at it, boys."

"According to the rules, Trace, you need to come with us to the tech area to observe," Johnny said. With that, he accelerated down pit row.

Trace shrugged and stepped out into the cooling night air. Tyler and Patrick were busy loading the Street Stock; Patrick was too excited to notice Trace. Mel was there, too, listening to Patrick talk on; she saw Trace, but turned her back.

And she wasn't the only one. Walking alone to the tech area, Trace passed a shadowy gauntlet of stares.

Other drivers followed him with their eyes, then turned away. Crew members muttered to one another, or laughed harshly.

Ahead, the blue Super Stock was surrounded by gawkers and the tech crew.

"Here, Trace," Johnny said. He tossed Trace a small camp stool from the ATV's toolbox. "You might as well get comfortable."

Trace sat down to watch as four tech guys, using tools from a tall box on wheels, took apart his engine. The intake manifold was already off. Next came the heads, which they took to the WISSOTA trailer for measurements. Trace knew the rule book. They would measure valve seats and other clearances. They would look for signs of porting—that is, polishing or grinding of the heads' inner chambers to increase airflow. Two guys used micrometers, bending over the brightly lit table as if doing an autopsy. Back at the car, two more tech guys worked on the lower end of the engine. Gerry Harkness held a trouble light for them.

"They have to take out one rod and piston," Johnny said. There was faint note of regret in his voice, as if to say, "No one wanted this to happen."

"Go for it," Trace threw back. The onlookers stood as silently as if they were gawkers at an accident site. Jimmy slipped into the crowd, cell phone in hand, as the tech guys worked. The glow from the phone's little screen lit up his narrow face and small eyes. Every couple of minutes his thumbs rapidly worked the letters, the numbers: reports to Smoky.

Tyler and Patrick came by with Trace's old car on the trailer. Patrick jumped out and hurried over. Tyler remained in his truck. "What's going on?" Patrick asked loudly.

No one said anything; the crowd all stared at him.

"Don't worry about it," Trace said to him. "Take my car home. I'll talk to you later."

Trace looked over at Tyler, who turned away and pretended to be occupied with the radio. Soon Patrick and Tyler were gone, and across the track, only the die-hard fans, the ones who knew about the protest, remained in the grandstands. Some of them gathered below the announcer's booth, waiting for the news. The moon tracked slowly upward behind thin clouds; there were no stars out. The pits quieted but for the clank and clatter of tools on the Super Stock, and the occasional sharp curses from the tech guys as their bare hands touched hot engine parts.

His phone beeped: his mother.

"Hey," Trace said.

"You were going to call me," she said. "How did you do tonight?"

"Second place," Trace answered. He turned away from the crowd.

"That's wonderful!" she said. "And guess what?"

"What?"

"I'm coming to see you race tomorrow night at Buffalo River Speedway."

"Great," Trace said evenly.

"I would have been there tonight, but under the circumstances — I mean, your father and Linda."

"Listen, I'm kinda in the middle of some things here," Trace said.

"Sure, honey. See you tomorrow night, okay?"

Trace closed his phone and returned to his camp stool. After a half hour more, the tech guys stood up, walked away from the Super Stock, and went into their trailer to confer. The jury was out.

"Don't worry, kid. Pizza's on me," Harlan said.

After several long minutes, the tech guys walked back to Trace and the Super Stock. Trace stood up. Harlan stepped forward to meet them — with an outstretched hand.

"Here you go," the chief pit steward said. He slapped the cash into Harlan's hand.

"Don't worry about putting my engine back together," Harlan said, nodding at the scattered parts along the fenders. "We prefer to do it ourselves."

"Believe me, we weren't going to," one of the tech guys said. His face was smudged and angry.

"Just to be clear, you found nothing illegal, right?" Harlan asked.

"That's right," the pit boss said.

"Loud and clear: nothing wrong?" Harlan said, looking around at the crowd.

"That's right, nothing wrong," the pit boss was forced to say, louder this time.

"But that's not the end of it," Johnny Walters said. "I've been racing twenty years, and I've never seen a Super Stock run like that."

"What he means is, they still think you're cheating," the chief pit steward said.

"Maybe you boys up here need to spend a little more time building your engines," Harlan said to the onlookers.

"Your check for second place is at the pit shack," Johnny said to Harlan. "Pick it up, and don't come back. Your team is not welcome here. Sorry, Trace," he added.

Trace set his jaw and said nothing.

"Don't worry. I wouldn't come back here to Flintstone Speedway if the purse was ten thousand to win," Harlan said.

Johnny looked at Trace, then drove away.

As the crowd dispersed, Jimmy gathered up the heads and the other parts scattered across the wide blue deck of the Super Stock. "I think there's some valves missing," he said.

"Forget about it," Harlan said. "Smoky's got more. Let's saddle up."

Trace headed back to his cabin. He was suddenly hungry, tired, and chilled from the night air. He looked out his little window at the now-empty pits, then turned away. He sat on his bed, then lay back on it and let out a long breath. Harlan started the big diesel engine, and soon, below, came the whir of the winch, then the thud and rocking motion of the Super Stock coming onboard.

After the big rear door clanged shut, air brakes hissed and the hauler began to move. Trace got up and looked out his window again. He watched as Headwaters Speedway—its old wreckers, its big and rusty water tank, the ancient water truck, the dark humps of bumper tires along the track, the pit shack, the tilted grandstand—passed by. There were still lights on in the announcer's booth—and suddenly a brighter glow flashed. Its door opened, and Mel stepped out to watch Trace's hauler pass.

He saw it from her eyes and his eyes, too: a train departing a station, one person standing on the platform, the other at the window of a train car. Neither of them waved, but then again it was too dark to see. As she passed out of sight into the shadows, Trace felt something dry up and crack in his heart.

His phone rang. It was Harlan. "You all right up there, kid?"

"Yes," Trace said. The hauler swayed sharply, then settled onto smoother blacktop.

"Don't worry about that engine protest thing," Harlan said.

"I wasn't," Trace said, still at his window as Headwaters Speedway shrank slowly behind him.

"Smoky's got us covered," Harlan continued. "We'll be good as new for tomorrow night at Buffalo River."

"I'll be ready," Trace said.

"That's the spirit," Harlan said. "By the way, that was some good driving, kid. You sure showed them."

"Yeah," Trace said, "I sure did."

He shut his phone to watch Headwaters disappear behind a dark wall of trees. It went away like a movie going to black. Afterward he lay down on his bed in the dark. He kept his eyes open. He listened to the diesel engine talk and the transmission, gear by smooth gear, reply as Harlan brought the hauler up to highway speed.

13

Trace awoke to sunlight in his side window. They were stopped; there was country music below in the trailer. Groggily he looked at his watch: 11:10 a.m.

"Hey, kid!" Harlan called as Trace appeared at his cabin door. "Thought we was going to have to call the undertaker."

"I'm alive," Trace said, and rubbed sleep from his eyes. Below, Smoky was bent over the Super Stock. A chain hoist, swaying slightly, dangled over the engine compartment; a new motor was in place.

"All good," came Jimmy's muffled voice from underneath the car. "Pressure plate is pressured, linkage is linked, bell housing is belled." He scooted out on his creeper, its steel wheels chattering across the diamond-tread floor. Last night's motor hung bolted to a stand; its vacant cylinders made it look like a giant, vee-shaped bug with eight eyeholes.

Trace blinked and shook his head to fully wake up. He scratched his jaw, raspy with whiskers. He would shave later—or not.

"You hungry?" Harlan called. "We stopped at the Golden Arches for a bag of breakfast."

"Yeah, thanks!" Trace said. He caught the bag as he came down the stairs.

Smoky glanced sideways through his sunglasses, then bent wider over the engine like a mother hen protecting a chick.

"Don't worry, I'm not going to look," Trace said.

Harlan and Jimmy cackled with laughter; Smoky mustered a small, twisted grin.

"I certainly wouldn't want to learn anything," Trace added.

Smoky continued to work on the motor while Trace sat there eating. This was some progress, anyway.

"Where are we, by the way?" Trace asked.

"At a rest stop just east of Fargo-Moorhead," Harlan said. "Pit gates don't open until two o'clock."

And they were not first at the gates. Buffalo River Speedway sat just north of Highway 10, the big east-west expressway, and when Team Blu rumbled in at one p.m., race car haulers were already lined up and waiting. It was the annual Sugar Beet Nationals, with good purses in all classes. The summer was slipping away quickly; drivers were hungry for national points.

"A real speedway," Harlan remarked as he looked around. "I like it."

By three o'clock, Team Blu was checked in, parked, and in full pre-race mode. Harlan worked with the new engine, making minor adjustments to the timing, letting Smoky listen to its rpm. Jimmy siped the tires with a hot iron, cutting fresh grooves diagonally across the treads. Tires were grooved according to specific tracks and specific conditions; Jimmy had brought into the trailer a big gob of Buffalo River clay, which he and Harlan squeezed and sniffed and examined like scientists. Now black rubber tailings smoked and fell from the tire as Jimmy worked.

"These would make good bass worms," Jimmy called to Trace, flicking a hot string of rubber Trace's way.

Wearing jeans and a sweatshirt, Trace sat in the sunlight off to the side in a lawn chair and watched the parade of arriving cars. Pure Stock beaters, their sides wrinkled but freshly painted. Cruiser cars with their double seats and gag decorations; one had a full-size Halloween skeleton riding in the rear, its skull bobbing. Lots of serious Modifieds. Quite a few Late Models and Super Stocks. Being at a newer, modernized speedway felt good. Being anonymous felt good, too. Last night at Headwaters was like a bad dream, the kind that took a while to go away. Just as he was making some progress on that, the Harkness school bus rolled in.

"Hey look, it's the Flintstones!" Harlan said to Jimmy, and pointed.

"Don't," Trace said.

Cindy Harkness gave Trace a brief nod as she geared the hauler slowly down pit row; Gerry Harkness, jaw set, pretended not to see Trace.

Trace got up and headed over to the concession area. On the way, he checked his cell phone. No calls from Mel, Patrick, or any of his other friends back home. He was also waiting to hear from his mother, who was en route; he had left a pit pass for her. Tasha, Carlos, and Laura were also due in; they were flying to Fargo, then driving out to the speedway with some kind of news. He thought of calling Sara Bishop just to say hello—he could use a friend tonight—but didn't. Her Super Stock was broke down, so he didn't expect to see her here.

The tidy concession area beneath the grandstand had no barbecue Waggin or chicken shack. Instead, a dozen or so kids and adults, mostly female, dressed in speedway T-shirts, hustled back and forth in the modern, clattering kitchen behind. There were several service windows. All food choices being equal, Trace chose the window with the cutest girl.

"Yes?" the cheerful blonde said to him. Her face was flushed from the heat in the kitchen; her hair was up, like Mel wore hers, with a ponytail poking through the back of her speedway cap.

"Any barbecued pork?" Trace asked. "I didn't see it on the menu."

"No pork. I've got brats and sloppy joes—that sort of thing." She smiled briefly. Her name tag read APRIL.

"Taco in a bag?"

"I can do that," she said.

He watched as she turned away, slit open a bag of corn chips, crunched its contents with a quick blow from wooden mallet, then poured in sloppy joe meat, shredded lettuce, tomatoes, cheese, and sour cream. Her fingers, white in transparent plastic gloves, moved quicker than minnows in a stream.

"You a driver?" she asked, not looking up.

"Yes," Trace said. "How'd you guess?"

"They always eat early, or else after the races, plus they have that beard stubble thing." She glanced back at him and smiled.

Trace touched the prickly side of his face. "You'd make a good detective."

"A better lawyer," she said, plopping a big spoonful of red taco sauce into the bag.

"A lawyer?" Trace asked. "That's, like, eight years of college after high school."

She looked up at him. "Six. I'm a junior at UND."

"Oh. Sorry," Trace said.

She smiled. "Don't worry about it. I've always looked young."

"Well, not that young," Trace fumbled. His eyes, with little brains of their own, scanned down her front, which was full and firm.

"How about you?" she asked, peeling off her gloves to

take Trace's ten-dollar bill. She brushed back a strand of curly, damp hair.

"How about me what?"

"What are your plans—to be the next Kasey Kahne?"

"The next Tony Stewart, maybe," Trace said.

"That guy's *really* annoying," April said as she made change.

"On the track maybe. He's probably a nice guy otherwise."

She glanced over Trace's shoulder; he could feel people close behind in line. "So what do you drive?" she asked.

"A Super Stock. The blue 18x."

Her eyebrows went up. "That big blue hauler that came in?"

Trace nodded.

"If I get a break, I'll try to catch a couple of laps," she said.

"That would be nice," Trace said. Their eyes met.

She smiled, then looked behind him. "Next!" she said.

At four-thirty, Trace's mother called. She was at the pit gate; she had her pass, but was unsure of where to go, what to do. He hurried to meet her. Her thin face broke into a smile as he approached, and she hugged him hard—which he didn't mind.

"You made it," he said.

"Yes. It's a long drive," she said loudly. She had already inserted her foam earplugs.

"Sorry about the miles," he replied.

"No, it's okay," she said quickly. "I'd rather come here. You know . . ."

"Over this way," Trace said, taking her arm; he didn't want to get into the whole parent thing.

She stuck close to his side as they walked along pit row—flinching as race cars tested their engines in bursts of rpm. She covered her nose at the sweet smell of 110-octane race fuel. As they passed Gerry Harkness, who was standing with several other drivers, Trace's mom said, "I feel like I know that guy."

"Let's keep going," Trace said, and steered her along. When he glanced backward over his shoulder, Gerry and the group of drivers all looked away.

"Here we are," Trace said, as they approached the Team Blu hauler.

She drew up to stare. "Are you serious?"

"Very," Trace said.

Harlan looked up from the Super Stock. "You must be Trace's mom?"

"That's right. Sharon."

"Pleased to meet you, Sharon," Harlan said, wiping his hands on a clean rag, then stepping forward. As they shook hands, he said, "I can sure see where this boy got his good looks."

Trace's mom actually blushed.

"Come on, I'll show you around," Trace said to her.

She was speechless at the trailer, the cabin, the car, the whole bustling speedway scene. "Like I said, I really feel dumb," she murmured as she looked around. "I just never took racing seriously."

His mother suddenly looked tired. "You've been driving all day," Trace said. "Why don't you have a nap in my cabin? There's plenty of time before the heats."

She let out a breath. "Maybe I will," she said.

Not ten minutes after Trace got his mother settled in, Tasha, Carlos, and Laura came riding down pit row on a speedway courtesy golf cart.

Carlos's voice chirped above the race car engines. Laura signaled the driver, a pit row dust bunny, to pull in by Team Blu. When the kid stopped, she peeled off a bill. He stared at the money with a confused look.

"It's for you," Tasha said. The kid's smudged face broke open into a white-toothed grin.

Laura was already headed toward the trailer. "Hi, guys!" she called cheerily. She wore her signature bright red lipstick.

"Be careful!" Harlan said, with a nod inside toward Trace's cabin. "He's got a woman in there."

Laura stopped. Jimmy cackled. Tasha frowned at Trace—who shrugged apologetically. Smoky laughed hoarsely from behind his window screen.

"He's a decent driver, but a real ladies' man," Harlan added.

"*Any*way," Laura said, turning her back on the stairway to Trace's cabin, "I'm here with very good news. Mr. Rupert came through with the budget we need, so we're here tonight to get some videotape and some more stills for our marketing peeps. We're gearing up to launch our campaign! I'll be talking with the speedway owner here about special promotions—how that all works in the racing world. Our goal is for Team Blu to be here, there, and everywhere real soon."

"Whoa," Jimmy said, excitement in his voice.

Laura looked at Jimmy, Harlan, and Trace. "You're going to be rolling down the freeway, and look out your window and see Trace and the car on billboards—billboards as big as that grandstand. Are you all ready for that?" She was pumped.

"Yahoo!" Jimmy said, with a short rebel yell.

Harlan nodded. "We're gonna blow doors off wherever we go."

"Second place last night," Laura said to Trace. "Not bad."

He was surprised that she knew, but shouldn't have been. "Thanks." He glanced at Harlan.

"A checkered flag would be perfect tonight," Laura said. "No pressure, of course!" she added.

Trace didn't laugh. "We'll do what we can."

"Great." Laura looked down pit row. "Carlos—we need pictures of all this!" she said, but Carlos was already snapping away. She turned back to Trace. "Why aren't you in your racing suit?"

Trace stared.

"He's one of those drivers who don't like to strut his stuff," Harlan said.

"Well, get over that," Laura said. "That's why we hired

you. I want you suited up the minute you arrive at a speed-way. Got that?"

"Okay," Trace said flatly.

"And I love the whiskers," she said, touching his chin. "Let's keep those."

Trace turned toward his cabin—where his mother stood in the open doorway. She had been listening.

"This is my mom," he announced. What could have been a funny moment—her appearance as "the woman"—now was not funny at all.

"Hi there," Sharon said as she came down the stairs.

"Very pleased to meet you," Laura said; suddenly she was all sweetness.

Trace's mom shook hands, but had no reply to Laura. With Tasha and Carlos, she smiled politely.

"We were just doing some business. Hope we didn't disturb you," Laura said.

"No problem," Sharon said. She kept staring at Laura.

"Okay, then," Laura said to Carlos. "Let's go get some photos. We'll talk!" she said to Sharon.

An announcement for Super Stocks came over the pit loudspeaker, and Trace was happy to suit up and climb into the car. Laura, Tasha, Carlos, and Sharon headed over to the stands to watch, which was also fine by Trace. He let Harlan straighten his belts and neck collar. Being in the cockpit always felt right. Felt good. It was a one-person space—his space. There was no room for adults and their issues, and the rules were simple and clear: go fast, turn left.

For a quarter-mile oval, the Buffalo River track had long straightaways, which left the corners tight, high, and sharply banked. He liked it immediately—or maybe it was the Red River Valley sticky black gumbo. The dark clay was tacky but firm; when he snapped the pedal down, the Super Stock jumped forward like a horse butt-shot by a BB gun. Lots of torque, lots of bite from the tires, but this engine felt 500 rpm flatter than last night's motor.

Back in the pits after hot laps, Trace tossed his helmet to Harlan, and pulled himself out. "I don't have a lot of top-end power," he said.

Harlan glanced at Jimmy, who looked at Smoky's window.

"You have enough," Smoky's voice croaked through the screen.

Trace shrugged. "If you say so."

His heat, the second of three for the Super Stocks, got off to a rough start. With an okay draw (number 29), he started third row outside. He knew better than to pass on the outside in turn 2, but tried anyway. A beat-up white local Super Stock, second row outside, swung his butt just wide enough to whack Trace's left front wheel—and push him high and squirrelly. Clearly this was one of Gerry Harkness's buddies. As Trace struggled to stay out of the wall, cars streamed by him on the low side. After that, it was difficult to make up much ground, especially with this engine. He did what he could, reeling in two cars, to finish seventh of nine.

As Trace rumbled into the pits, Harlan gestured like a

traffic cop. "Bring it inside!" he called, and pointed to the trailer.

Trace turned the nose toward the open hauler, then lurched upward onto the ramp and inside. He pulled himself out through the window. "The top end is just not there!"

"Not to worry," Harlan said. "Smoky will look at it." He nodded to Jimmy, who was already closing the hauler door. "In private," Harlan added.

Wearing his racing suit, Trace headed over to the stands for the other heats. As he climbed the bleachers toward the Team Blu group and his mother, two small tweeny girls rushed up to block his way. "Could you sign our program?" they asked, giggling.

"Sure," he said. Glancing up, he saw Carlos snapping away with his camera.

"That was sweet," Laura said as he approached.

"Now you have to win for sure," Tasha said as Trace settled in between Laura and his mother.

In the twenty-lap feature, No. 18x was a different car. Smoky had worked some kind of magic on the motor. As Trace rolled around the track under the pre-race yellow, he popped the gas pedal again and again; it barked back at him like a bullwhip cracking. The Super Stocks fell in, two wide, for the green-flag lap. Trace made sure to breathe, and waggled his fingers on the wheel in order to stay loose.

In the ninth row outside, which put him in eighteenth position among the twenty-four cars, Trace tucked in tight against the car ahead. He tapped his butt to send a message. He rode him close, nudging, bumping—everyone did it—toward green-flag thunder.

When the convoy of Super Stocks exploded forward, Trace hammered down and cranked the wheel toward a high side. There were always more options on the outside. On the other hand, a high line made for a longer track—but that was offset by Trace's engine and setup. He couldn't believe how much bite he had in the rear tires— thank you, Jimmy! Passing three cars on the high side, he stayed up in the corners—dangerously close to the marbles—and let the car do its work. Within three laps he was running in the middle of the pack, and looking for holes as the cars started to string out.

On the second yellow-flag restart, Trace rolled somewhere around tenth. At track level, the dust made it difficult for a driver to see car placement—way harder than for spectators. But the restart was now single-file, which simplified things plus gave him more room to move. At the green flag, the car in front swung upward to block Trace's line (his fast groove up high had not gone unnoticed). Trace guessed correctly and dove low, streaming past a couple of Gerry Harkness's friends who were not quick enough to pinch off Trace's line or box him in. Gerry himself had faded to the rear.

By lap 16 (Buffalo River had a flashing lap counter sign in the infield by turn 1), Trace was in fourth place. The tight group of four was well-matched. Each had good power; each had his setup right. It was just a question of who would make a mistake.

The bright green No. 77 and the red No. 62 had some kind of personal grudge thing going on—they traded sheet metal in every turn—tap and tap back. Trace zeroed in on them. Sure enough, on turn 4 of lap 18, the two cars bumped hard enough to knock each other loose—which was when Trace threaded the needle. He cut between them, and an instant later heard them slam back together like a giant pincers closing. They staggered, kept their lines, but fell sharply off the pace.

Trace concentrated on the leader, the black No. 707 driven by Ryan O'Hare, the current Super Stock points leader. With power to spare, Trace came up hard behind him. O'Hare swung his tail to the right just enough to keep Trace there. White flag: one lap to go.

Trace took a higher line, and decoyed O'Hare gradually upward. On the last lap, turn 3, Trace gambled by tapping his brakes. No. 707 surged ahead—but Trace dove low and got him on the inside. Drifting perfectly parallel through the last turn, the two Super Stocks came nose to nose down the stretch. Trace's engine, at redline rpm, pulled him underneath the checkered flag by half a car length.

Pounding the wheel, he let loose a rebel yell of his own. There was no stopping this car, and no stopping him, either. But then he focused on getting to the scales.

There was always a moment, as the car swayed gently

on the boards, and as the tech guy did the weigh-in thing, of doubt and fear. But when the weight shack guy waved him forward, Trace let out another whoop. Off the boards, he spun a cloud of dust as he headed to the victory circle.

Buffalo River had a real trophy girl—no little kids here—wearing a skimpy T-shirt. She leaned close to Trace as cameras flashed. "Hey, new guy in town," she said, all the while smiling at the lenses, "great driving!"

"Thanks!"

"I don't bite, put your arm around me!" she said. She kept a fixed smile.

Trace obeyed, and the cameras flashed again. The announcer was making a big deal about Trace's first feature win in a Super Stock. The Team Blu members, along with Trace's mom, waved wildly from behind the wire-mesh fence.

After receiving the trophy, Trace burned a donut, then headed to the tech lane. This time, the inspection was brief, after which he headed to the pits.

Harlan and Jimmy stood in front of the ramp, backs to him, talking. Trace came up fast behind; they appeared not to notice him.

"Hey!" Trace shouted. "You want to get run over?"

They turned with fake surprise. "Did you race already?" Harlan asked.

"Oh man, we missed it, Pops!" Jimmy said. "We was over in the concessions getting some cotton candy."

"Very funny," Trace called. He barked the motor one

last time, then hit the kill switch. Harlan, then Jimmy, busted up laughing. They laughed so hard they had to sit down.

"So how'd you do, anyway?" Harlan asked.

Jimmy started laughing all over again. Behind the motor home window screen, Smoky croaked like a bull-frog.

"Let's see," Trace said, as he tossed his helmet to Harlan and pulled himself through the window. "I think it was fifteenth, or maybe twentieth—I forget. But, whoa—what have we here?" He reached in the cockpit and pulled out the tall trophy.

"Sweet!" Jimmy said.

At that moment, the rest of Team Blu arrived. Trace made sure to hug his mother first and Carlos last, with Tasha and Laura in between.

"Made to order," Carlos said excitedly, "and all on videotape!"

"Perfect!" Laura said, one arm still around Trace.

"There's a girl over by the grandstand gate who says she knows you," Trace's mom said.

Trace looked up and squinted through the glare of the pit lights glinting off race cars and haulers. It was Sara. She waved excitedly.

"Excuse me," Trace said to the crew, and walked quickly away.

"What did I tell you?" Sara called as he approached. She grinned broadly. "I knew you were a winner."

Trace smiled and stepped through the gate. They had a nice long hug.

"I would have come over earlier, but I couldn't afford a pit pass," Sara said apologetically as she released him.

"Hey, I'm just glad you came!" Trace said. "After last night, I kinda need a friend."

"That was a mess," Sara said. "I feel bad about your friend, Melody—and then your teardown. Jeez."

"Hey, that was last night," Trace said. "All behind me."

"Melody, too?" Sara asked.

Trace paused—just as a cluster of little kids, mostly boys, hurried up to him. "Trace! Trace! Can you sign my program? You got any driver cards? Can I have one?"

"Whoa," Trace said as the kids bumped against him.

Sara laughed. "I can't hang out," she said. "But stay in touch?"

"For sure!" Trace said. Then she disappeared in the crowd.

It took him a few minutes with the kids, and when he was finally done, he turned to go back to the pits. For some reason he looked into the shadows, alongside the bleachers. Leaning against the metal wall was April. She was watching him and smiling.

"Hey," he said, and walked over.

"Some driving," she said.

"Thanks," he said.

She stepped very close. He could smell food on her: sweet corn, butter, taco sauce, cotton candy. She touched his face. "I could punch out anytime," she murmured.

Trace swallowed. "Gee, um. That would be great—except that I've got a bunch of people here—sponsors and . . ."

"And?" April asked. She let her hand track slowly down across his chest; her fingers touched the zipper on his racing suit.

Trace started to laugh. "And my mother."

April smiled. "Just my luck!" she said.

"Hey, you don't look like the kind of girl who needs any luck," Trace said. He glanced around, then pulled her sharply forward and kissed her. She melted against him. The small of her back was damp and warm. Her front, hard against his chest, left him speechless.

"Trust me, I smell a lot better when I've had a shower," she whispered as they kissed again.

"You smell great to me," Trace murmured, his voice suddenly hoarse with desire.

Someone cleared his throat not far away. It was Jimmy, standing with his thumbs hooked in his pockets, and looking off toward the freeway. "Uh, the Team Blu gang needs you," he said, as if talking to the passing headlights.

"Coming," Trace said.

April pulled a pen, a Sharpie, from somewhere; she opened his right hand, wrote her telephone number on the inside of his palm, then curled his fingers over it. "Indelible ink," she said. "It won't wash off." She gave him a last quick peck on the cheek, and walked away.

———

It always took a while to unwind after a race, but it took longer tonight. Trace said goodbye to his mother, who had a motel in Moorhead, and to the Team Blu corporate folks, who had theirs in Fargo. After that he called his dad, and then Patrick—who could be depended upon to tell Mel. Patrick answered with the voices of other teenagers chattering in the background; he sounded strange—like he was unable to talk freely. Trace realized that Mel was nearby. They were at a party of some kind. "That's the news," Trace said abruptly. "I gotta go."

But he didn't, really. He had nowhere to go. Everyone was gone except for Harlan and Jimmy and Smoky, clattering around in the trailer below as they buttoned up the Super Stock. He took a hot shower to try to relax, and shaved as well. Afterward he felt clean, but still edgy. He thought of calling April—or maybe not April, but Sara. Or maybe not Sara, but Mel—just to hear her voice. He punched in her number before he lost his nerve. It rang four times. Then her voice mail clicked on. He listened to her voice, but couldn't think of any message.

He shut his phone and leaned against his door, waiting. Hoping she would call back. Then someone's heavy feet came up his stairs, followed by a sharp rap on his door. Holding his cell phone, he opened the door.

"Schedule update," Harlan said, handing Trace a printout. "And by the way—good driving tonight. Hardly got a chance to tell you."

Trace looked down at the sheet.

"Sioux Falls, South Dakota, tomorrow night, and Aberdeen the next," Harlan said.

Trace's gaze went from the schedule back to his cell phone. He held it up—stared at it—waiting for it to ring. But it didn't. It lay in his palm as silent as a brick. He waited a few more seconds, then put the phone in a back pocket.

"Okay," he said to Harlan. "Let's go racing."